This special signed edition
is limited to 2000 copies.

This is copy

1767

The Road
to
Lisdoonvarna

A Mystery

The Road
to
Lisdoonvarna
A Mystery

Charles de Lint

Subterranean Press · 2001

FIRST EDITION
May 2001

ISBN
1-892284-91-x

Subterranean Press
P.O. Box 190106
Burton, MI 48519

email:
publish@subterraneanpress.com

website:
www.subterraneanpress.com

for
Rodger

a hardboiled bear
with a softboiled heart

Introduction

I've always had eclectic tastes, even as a teenager. I don't know why. I wanted to fit in as much as the next person, but my reading and listening tastes kept straying into uncool (if intriguing to me) regions, and continue to do so to this day. Happily, for that teenager I was, the hippies arrived in the mid-sixties and the most diverse forms of books and music became of great fascination to all.

But even then, I suppose I bucked the trend. Sure, I enjoyed the writing of the new and old Beats, the music of the British Invasion and West Coast psychedelia. But even in those days of peace, love and flowers I was still fascinated by the hardboiled detective novel and remain so to this day. Today I might be reading Andrew Vachss and Dennis Lehane rather than Mickey Spillane, but the love of the form has never left me.

So while I love writing fantasy—especially its intriguing off-shoot mythic fiction[1]—it's probably not so surprising that

---

[1] This is a term coined by Terri Windling to describe stories that deal with the relationships characters have with each other, with themselves, and with the world in which they live that use mythological and folkloric material either as a resonating mirror, or to illuminate those same concerns by allowing interior landscapes and emotional states to appear physically "on stage" with what most would consider more realistically portrayed elements. (For a longer discussion on this subject, you should visit Terri's website at www.endicott-studio.com.)

I'd eventually try my hand at a mystery novel, and that's just what I did in the mid-eighties when I began the book you now hold in your hands.

I've flirted with variations on the form in other books. *Mulengro, Angel of Darkness* and *From a Whisper to a Scream* (the latter two first published under the pen name of Samuel M. Key) were all, at their heart, police procedurals, sparked mostly, I'd guess, from years of reading Ed McBain. I'd also touched on spy thrillers (the RCMP sections of *Moonheart*), tropes such as organized crime (the Mafia in *Greenmantle*), and various hardboiled characters who've shown up in the pages of various novels and stories (*Moonheart*'s Blue and *Someplace to Be Flying*'s Hank Walker come most immediately to mind, though you'll also find such characters sprinkled through the short stories in the Newford collections).

But this was the first time that I sat down to deliberately write a mystery novel, with a PI as a lead character, and no fantasy elements whatsoever, hedging my bets only slightly by giving Jevon "Jake" Swann a love for Celtic music. (It doesn't matter where you put Celtic music; it always holds a touch of magic to it.) And then I set the story in Ottawa, because that's where I was living at the time and I liked having my characters walk around in the same neighbourhoods that I did, or could.

So, to keep this introduction relatively short, after nine or ten months of writing, I had myself a mystery novel. Now what to do with it?

My agent at the time wasn't particularly enthused with it—but that same agent didn't really care for *Trader,* later on, so I now take his critique with a large grain of salt, since I was very happy with *Trader.* And to be fair, it's hard to sell an author strongly associated with one genre to another. I think it went out to one publishing house, got turned down, and then nothing much happened with it afterwards.

My agent didn't consider it a priority and by that time I was well into *Drink Down the Moon* and getting more excited with my extensive research for *Svaha,* so it went into a file cabinet and was forgotten until Bill Schafer and I got talking one day about my doing a novel for him. At the time he was asking for something very different from what I'd published to date and the first thing that came to my mind was *The Road to Lisdoonvarna.*

Unlike my other recent Subterranean Press book, *Triskell Tales,* where part of the point was to show the evolution of a storyteller learning his craft so only typographical errors were corrected, I've rewritten *The Road to Lisdoonvarna.* Not extensively, because that would be too much like rewriting another person's book and perhaps losing that indefinable something that lies in between the lines. (How well do you know the person you were sixteen years ago?) And I also wanted to retain the flavour of the eighties that lies in its pages – the decade most of us want to forget with its disco and bad fashions and all.

(I know disco music is enjoying something of a comeback, but really. Have you ever noticed that the movies made in the seventies and eighties don't date nearly as well as those of previous decades? It's the clothes, mostly, though partly the dialogue and music. I went through those decades being completely out-of-fashion in my long hair, my jeans and Indian cotton shirts, and when I look at those movies, I'm happy I did. But I digress.)

I remember having a great time writing *The Road to Lisdoonvarna.* And being pleasantly surprised coming back to it after all these years. It's not like what I write now, or like the contemporary and secondary world fantasies I wrote before it, but there's still a family resemblance.

I was also surprised by a couple of things.

Reading *The Road to Lisdoonvarna* over prior to my rewrite for this edition, I remember thinking that my influences would certainly be showing in its pages. Robert Crais, for sure. Probably Andrew Vachss. But I began the manuscript in 1984 and completed it in early 1985. Crais's first book, *The Monkey's*

Raincoat, didn't come out until 1987. The first Vachss was *Flood,* which came out in 1985 when I was finishing the book up. So I suppose, unless I was momentarily gifted with the ability to literally read the future, we have to look back at all those earlier mysteries and spy thrillers I was reading.

The other was that I didn't know how the story was going to turn out. I found myself turning pages to find out what happened next — which is a good thing, of course, because part of the fun of a mystery novel is trying to guess how it will all work out.

Here's hoping you have a similar experience.

— Charles de Lint
Ottawa, Winter 2001

As life runs on, the road grows strange
With faces new, and near the end
The milestones into headstones change...

—James Russell Lowell,
from "Sixty-eighth Birthday"

Chapter One

At least she was still alive.

A day, a week from this moment, that might not be enough, but for now it was all she had. It was all they had left her after they were done.

And she knew where she was.

They had dumped her in the little square of a park on Murray Street near the corner of Sussex Drive. Hookers strutted by on the sidewalk, a parade of high heels, fishnet stockings, tight pants and swaying hips. Johns cruised Murray in their cars, some just window shopping, others parked and haggling over the price after they'd made their choices. On the park benches the pimps sat, calling encouragement and abuse to their girls, occasionally jotting down the license plates of the cars they got into. Mostly they were just talking to each other about the kind of money their girls were bringing in, smoking endless cigarettes and joints, sharing the odd bottle.

No one paid any attention to her. The hookers were working. The johns weren't interested in someone in her shape. The pimps didn't care.

She didn't try to stand.

Her face was bruised, lips split and bleeding, nose broken. Every breath hurt. There were ribs cracked, if not broken. When she breathed, she could only take quick short breaths. Her lungs burned, her whole chest felt constricted. The air going by the open nerve of a broken tooth was a constant raw pain. Lower down, vaginal cramps spasmed, even when she didn't try to move. The crotch of her sweatpants was wet with blood.

They'd left her leaning up against the brick wall of the building that backed the east side of the tiny park, half-hidden in the shadows. She knew she had to get to a hospital. Knew that no one was going to help her unless she got right out onto the street where they couldn't ignore her.

It was all she could do to crawl.

She made little mewling sounds as she dragged herself to the sidewalk. A man walked by and looked down at her distastefully. By the time she reached the pavement, another man was passing. He wore a neat white cotton suit and a blue-flowered shirt open at the throat.

"Jesus," he said as she lifted a bloody hand towards him. "I just got this suit, fercrissakes."

He circled widely around her and continued down the sidewalk. The "please help me" she'd been trying to shape stayed in her throat. She knew she wouldn't be able to speak the words anymore. All she could do was vomit them up.

Being alive wasn't going to be enough.

She lay half on, half off the sidewalk, her face pressed against the pavement, and closed her eyes. Someone had stopped and was standing over her now, but whatever strength she'd had left after her ordeal had been spent. Besides, what did it matter? Nobody wanted to get involved. Nobody cared. She wasn't sure if she even cared anymore.

She just let her mind go drifting.

Ireland.

She'd always wanted to go to Ireland, but she hadn't made it yet. County Clare and the festival they held there in the village of Lisdoonvarna every summer. All the best traditional Irish musicians gathered there, all the top bands. She'd wanted to be there, with her fiddle under her arm, and sit down in a pub or on a street corner and just play tunes with her heroes.

Micho Russell. Christy Moore. Paddy Glackin. All the rest of them.

To hear that music. A bodhran rattling a rhythm against the wailing of the pipes and fiddles. A tin whistle skirling high above them all. Maybe Jackie Daly would be sitting in, fingers dancing on the buttons of his accordion.

She could almost hear it.

Twenty-seven years old and she'd never done the one thing she'd always said she was going to do. It wasn't that it was important to anyone but her. It wasn't going to save the world. It wasn't going to solve the famines in Ethiopia, or the cruise missile crisis, or Star Wars, or unemployment, or the war in Lebanon. But it was something she'd always wanted to do. It sure beat lying here, maybe dying.

The wail of a siren mixed with the music in her imagination, but she still refused to move or even open her eyes. It wouldn't be an ambulance coming for her. Anybody seeing her here would just think that she was a hooker herself. They'd figure that her pimp had beaten her up and wouldn't want to get mixed up in it. Nobody was going to help her, so she just let herself go.

She went to Lisdoonvarna. She saw Finbar Furey playing his Uillean pipes, his big hands moving like quicksilver over the holes and on the shiny keys of his chanter. Somebody asked him, "Why do you play so fast?" and he answered, "Because I can."

Why was she lying here?

Because she could.

Because she couldn't do anything else.

Right now, this was something she was good at. Just lying here, hurting. Oh God, how she was hurting.

The narrow streets of Lisdoonvarna slipped away. The music faded. There were hands under her, lifting her gently onto a stretcher, but she could barely feel them. She kept trying to recapture that village in the west of Ireland, to hear the music again, but it all dissolved into oblivion.

It was early evening. The air conditioning was on, its dull hum competing with the Lionel Ritchie album playing on the stereo. The kitchen was lit by a hanging lamp. An eight-by-ten inch mirror lying flat on the table reflected the brightness back up to the ceiling. On the surface of the mirror was a small neat mound of white powder, a razor blade and the two short lines of the powder that the blade had scraped together. Beside the mirror was a set of scales and a plastic bag with a light detritus of the same white powder coating its inner surface.

Occupying one of the four chairs set around the table, Paul King grinned to himself.

He was alone in the kitchen, alone with his treasure. Uncut, Rocko had assured him. Pure Colombian snow. Which meant it was maybe seventy percent, tops.

He'd see. It was one thing taste-testing the stuff on your tongue with Rocko and one of his goons standing nearby. Watching. Waiting. The blow had checked out pretty good then, and Rocko had never ripped him off before, but Paul always liked to wait until this moment to be absolutely sure what kind of deal he'd scored. Alone in the apartment, Ritchie crooning from the stereo's speakers, the coke all laid out on the mirror, sparkling and pretty...

This was the moment.

Leaning forward, he pressed the index finger of his left hand against one nostril and snorted the first line through a short plastic straw up the other.

Then he sat back.

His eyes began to water almost immediately. The inner membrane of his nose and the back of his throat went pleasantly numb. Rocko had stepped on it, he decided. But not much. Not much at all. Not half as much as Paul would himself.

He leaned forward again and took the other line up his left nostril, then laid the straw down on the mirror. Definitely worth the two grand.

He wet his finger, swept up the grains he'd missed and rubbed them into his gums. Damn fine. Humming along with Ritchie's "Hello," he went over to the sink and rinsed his nostrils. Can't be too careful. His customers could walk around with runny noses all they liked, but not him. He knew just how much to take and how often. Even as high as he was right at this moment, he was still in control. That was what was important. The control.

He dried his nose. Tossing the towel onto the counter, he returned to the table.

He had the same control with his dealing. Everybody wanted their blow, but he only dealt with people he knew. His clients knew that if they had a new customer for him, they had to clear it with him first. Paranoid, maybe, but he'd been in the business for years now and he planned to stay in it.

It didn't pay to get too greedy. He kept the amount he dealt at a certain constant level and the number of his clients was fixed. He'd seen others in the business burn themselves out, always trying to expand too much, too quickly, until it got out of hand and they either went down or got busted. That was *not* going to happen to Paul King.

The door buzzer sounded and he glanced at his watch as he went down the hall. Billy was early tonight. Probably wanted to catch him before he stepped on the coke. Billy liked his blow as pure as he could get it. He was the only customer Paul allowed to make a pick up. Paul charged him a little more for the privilege, but Billy didn't seem to mind.

Last delivery Paul had already stepped on it before Billy showed up, which was probably why he was coming by early tonight. Paul didn't think he stepped on it too much. You had to make your bread and most people didn't know the difference anyway. Billy was one of the few that did.

"Hey, Billy," he began as he opened the door.

The rest of what he'd been about to say died stillborn in his throat and all he could do was stand there, staring stupidly at the big man who filled the doorway.

It wasn't Billy.

Paul's control fizzled and died as a rush of fear went through him. Cocky. Oh Jesus, he'd gotten too cocky. The shit was just lying there on the table. Jes-*sus*.

The man was a good six-two, weighing in at about one hundred and ninety pounds. He wore a rumpled blue suit, white shirt undone at the collar, tie hanging loose just below the opening. He had blond hair, dark brows. His chin was square, eyes blue. They were mean eyes. Cop eyes.

Paul took it all in, pulse drumming, knees going weak, bowels feeling a little loose.

"Paul King?" the man asked.

Paul swallowed dryly and nodded.

The man flipped open his billfold to show Paul his badge. "Detective Marsh, Ottawa Police Department."

Paul sagged visibly. As the detective stepped inside, he backed slowly from the big man. He was slender, a half head shorter than the policeman and no match for him, but for one brief moment Paul envisioned himself smashing the cop against the wall and making a break for it. Then common sense prevailed. A break to where? Everything he had was in this place.

"You need…" He began. "Where's your warrant? I've got rights…"

It all came out in a rush, none of it really making sense. The detective flipped his billfold closed with a practiced motion and stowed it away in the inner pocket of his suit jacket. He continued to move down the short hall, forcing Paul ahead of him, until they were in the kitchen. The detective smiled.

"I've got the warrant right here," he said, patting his jacket.

Trembling, Paul pulled out a chair and sank weakly into it. He stared numbly at the cocaine. This was it. He was finished. The same coke that had been making him feel so good earlier was working against him now. It lay there on the table — plain evidence. It clouded up his mind so that he couldn't think straight. He'd visualized getting busted before — worked out what he'd do, how he'd handle it — but now he'd let the fear get hold of him and it wouldn't let go long enough for him to think straight.

The detective stood over him. Wetting a finger, the detective touched it to the cocaine. He shook his head as he withdrew his finger from his tongue.

"Nice bit of nose candy you've got here, King," he said. "Now why don't you tell me where you got it."

He sat down across from Paul and proceeded to scrape the coke into the plastic bag. He worked efficiently, tying a knot to close the bag when he was done, then dropping it into a side pocket.

Paul stared at the policeman's hands until the cocaine disappeared from sight. His gaze lifted until it met the detective's cold blue eyes.

Where'd he get it? His fear told him that he'd just make things worse for himself if he fingered Rocko, but if he could make a deal...

Nothing in the detective's eyes gave Paul a starting point.

"I, uh...I've got some bread," he said.

"How much?"

Paul blinked. He studied the detective again. In one brief moment the man had changed from an immovable force into something it was possible he could manipulate. Maybe he could buy his way out of this. How much did he have in his stash? A grand? Fifteen hundred? He couldn't remember. How much would it take to buy the sucker off? Maybe he could get away with five hundred.

He named that amount.

The detective tapped his fingers on the table, then smiled.

"Let's see where you've got it stashed," he said.

Oh Jesus, Paul thought. Was he dumb or what? Now the bastard was going to take it all. Except if it got him off, it'd be worth it — wouldn't it? Christ, he didn't need to even think about the answer to that. He'd pay a hundred times that amount if he had it, because there was no way he could go to jail. He just couldn't handle it.

"C'mon, pretty boy," the detective said. "Let's get a move on."

Paul went to the freezer and took out the bottom loaf of two. He brought it back to the table and handed it over to the cop.

"Cute," the detective said.

He opened the package and flipped through the slices of bread until he came to the hollowed-out middle of the loaf and the sheaf of brown one hundred dollar bills that had been hidden in the cavity. He counted them out. Seventeen hundred dollars.

"A little more than five bills here," the detective said.

Paul nodded. "Take it. Take it all."

The detective tapped the money against the palm of his hand, then laid it on the table.

"Oh, I will," he said finally. "But it's not going to be that easy."

"Jesus, man..."

"I want the name of whoever it was that sold you this. And don't fuck around with me — I know who's dealing blow and who isn't."

"I can't tell you that."

"We play this game my way, or we don't play it at all."

"What do you want his name for?"

"Why do you care?"

"He'll kill me."

The detective shook his head. "I won't tell him. Not unless you fuck up. I just want it for insurance. And you'd better not shit me, pretty boy, or things'll get really rough."

The seconds ticked by. Paul stared at the money lying between them on the table. The bastard. He had everything. The dope. The money. The badge.

"Okay," the detective said. "Time's up. I'm taking you downtown."

He stood up and Paul shrank back against his chair.

"Rocko," he said quickly. "Rocko Montalto. I swear it's true."

The detective studied him for a long moment, then nodded.

"Okay," he said finally. "It's Rocko."

He picked up the money and stuffed it into the same pocket that held the cocaine.

"I'll be keeping an eye on you, King," he added. "Fuck up and you've not only got me to worry about, but Rocko too. Understand?"

"You're not...you're not taking me in...?"

The detective shook his head. "We've got a deal now. But you're out of the business, pretty boy. Don't make me utilize options I don't want to have to use on you."

"Sure. Sure. I won't fuck up."

"I'll see myself out."

Paul sat there and cradled his head on the table, listening to the man leave. When Billy came by about fifteen minutes later, Paul sent him away and told him that he'd retired. The cocaine rush had let him down a long time ago by the time his roommate came home. He had a throbbing headache and barely looked up as Roddy came into the kitchen.

"Paul?"

He looked up to meet Roddy's worried features.

"Oh Jesus, Roddy," he said. "I came this close to getting busted."

Roddy sat down in the chair that the detective had vacated and took Paul's hand.

"What happened?" he asked.

Paul told him.

"C'mon," Roddy said when he was done. "It's not so bad. At least you're not in jail."

"But all that bread..."

"We never needed the money, Paul. We never needed any of the money you got from dealing. You know that. It was like a bad habit that you had to break."

"I guess."

"So what're you going to do now?"

"I don't have a whole lot of choice, do I?" Paul said. "I can't deal with Rocko now or that cop'll sic him on me, and I can't deal with anybody else because who is there I can trust? Besides, that cop said he'd be keeping tabs on me."

"We don't need that money," Roddy repeated.

Paul shrugged. It wasn't exactly the money, he'd realized a long time ago, but what went with it. The man with the blow — that's who he'd been. An important guy, a guy with connections. The whole dealing trip had added a certain exotic quality to his life for the very reason of its risk. But after tonight...

Christ, he'd come so close to losing it all.

"I guess we don't need it," he said.

Roddy smiled. "C'mon Paul. Let's hit the sack. You'll feel a whole lot better about it in the morning."

"Looks like its your turn to be strong," Paul said as he let himself be led down the hall.

Roddy nodded. He'd always been stronger, but he knew better than to say it aloud.

J

evon Swann had a special relationship with his answering service — one that he regretted every morning when the phone rang. Hooking the receiver free, he brought it up to his ear and stared blearily at the wall beside his bed that served as his appointment pad. There were two Scotch Post-its with messages on them stuck to the wall. He grunted into the mouthpiece.

"Good morning, Jake," came the too-cheerful reply. "Time to get up."

Swann rolled onto his back and stared at the ceiling. "You really enjoy this, don't you?"

"Just trying to do my job."

"How can anybody be so cheerful at this time of the morning?"

"It's nine-thirty, Jake. Everybody else is already up."

"On a Saturday?"

"You sound groggier than usual — what were you up to last night?"

"Not much. Thanks for the call, Sue. Any messages?"

"At this time of the morning?" she replied with a laugh. "I've got to go — there's someone on the other line. Have a nice day, Jake."

"Yeah. You, too."

He sat up against the headboard and cradled the receiver. Wake up, he told his body, but it was the same struggle every morning. Glancing at the Post-its, he pulled them free from the wall and studied them. Two appointments. The first was in half an hour.

Swinging his feet to the floor, he padded across the room to his stereo and inserted a cassette. A jaunty Scottish reel, written and performed on the accordion by Phil Cunningham, spilled from the speakers. Swann frowned. Everything was too cheerful in the morning. Leaving the tape playing, he went into the bathroom for a shave and a shower to cut through the fog.

Twenty minutes later he was ready to go. He started for the door, then paused and went back to his closet. From the pocket of a blue suit jacket he pulled a roll of hundred dollar bills and a small plastic bag filled with white powder. He flushed the cocaine down the toilet and pocketed the money. Taking the time to stuff a blonde wig and a plastic eye-contacts case into his top dresser drawer, he left the apartment.

———

The Avenue Restaurant was always crowded on a Saturday morning, but his usual table was free. It was a semi-circular booth, the only one like it in the restaurant. Situated down by the washrooms, it offered a certain amount of privacy from the other booths and tables. Swann had done The Avenue's owner a favour a couple of years back and ever since then the booth had been his. No one else used it until noon. Swann slid into the booth and the blonde waitress brought him a coffee without being asked.

"There's a guy here to see you," she said.

Swann glanced over to the counter and spotted his client straight off. Matching the trim grey suit and hang-dog features to the anxious, slightly pompous voice he'd spoken to on the phone yesterday wasn't hard.

"Thanks, Belle," he said, pulling the coffee over in front of him. "Send him over, would you?"

"Sure. You want some breakfast?"

Swann nodded. He watched Belle make her way back to the counter where she pointed Swann out to the waiting man. Grey-suit stood up and looked uncertain until Swann waved him over. He carried his coffee cup fastidiously as he approached Swann's table, careful not to spill a drop of the liquid into the saucer. Swann had the sudden urge to trip him.

"Mr. Swann…?"

"Sit down, Mr. Menzies," Swann said. He didn't stand up or offer his hand. "How can I help you?"

Menzies looked around the restaurant. "I'd rather discuss it in your office."

"This is my office."

Menzies blinked. Does a nice bird imitation, Swann thought.

"But where do you keep your files?" Menzies asked.

"I don't believe in paperwork."

"But—"

"Listen, Mr. Menzies. If you want a sheaf of paper outlining what's done and when every step of the way, maybe you should go with one of the big agencies. My fee's a flat seventy-five a day, plus expenses. I can get away with that because I favour the bare bones approach. All I do is get the job done."

"You seem very sure of yourself."

Swann leaned back and studied Menzies for a long moment. "Let's talk about your problem, Mr. Menzies."

"I…" Menzies began, then he nodded. "You came highly recommended—Arthur had nothing but good to say of you— so I shouldn't question your methods. Just so long as you, as you say, get the job done."

"Which is?" Swann prompted as Menzies lapsed into silence.

"It's my daughter, Mr. Swann. Trish—Patricia. She's disappeared."

"I don't really do missing persons—it takes too much legwork. Maybe you *should* try one of the agencies."

It was only half true. A missing persons case did take a lot of legwork and Swann did take them, he just didn't like them— not when they involved kids. When he was feeling flush after a job, which he was now, he liked to pick and choose what he took on next.

"I have tried an agency," Menzies said. "And the police. Neither of them brought her back."

"What makes you think I'll be any different?"

"Arthur said you know the city. He said that you can investigate avenues that are closed to the police and the agencies."

Swann shrugged, not wanting to commit himself to anything at this point. "How old is she?"

"Fifteen—or she was when she disappeared. She's turned sixteen in the interim."

"That makes her old enough to make her own choices."

"She's just a child still, Mr. Swann."

Daddy's little girl went and grew up too fast, Swann thought.

"How long ago did she disappear?"

"Three months now."

"That's some time. What makes you think she's in Ottawa?"

Menzies brought a postcard out from the inner pocket of his suit coat and passed it over. Swann glanced at the Mounties in full ceremonial dress on the front, then flipped it around to read the back. "I know you're worried," it said, "but this is just something I have to do. Please don't look for me. I'll be back when things make more sense. Love, Trish." It was postmarked a week ago in Ottawa.

"That's her handwriting?" he asked.

"Yes."

Swann read the card again. "Problems at home?" he tried.

"Nothing that would warrant her running away. Trish has always had her own ideas about things, but she's a good girl. She's always done what she was told."

Until she just couldn't take it anymore. It was an old, old story, Swann thought, given new life every time another kid realized that the world was crapping on them.

"Do you have a picture of her?"

Menzies handed him two photos. The first was of a pretty girl of perhaps thirteen or fourteen. She had a heart-shaped face, light brown hair worn in a loose shag cut, pouty lips. Real cheerleader material. It took Swann a moment or so to realize that the second photo was of the same girl.

The first had been a school photo — a head-and-shoulders shot, taken by a professional photographer. The girl had been wearing a rose-coloured angora sweater. The second was a snapshot. In it, she'd traded in the sweater for a torn T-shirt and a leather vest. Her head was shaved except for a spiked Mohawk that lifted a good five inches straight up from her skull. The spikes were a variety of colours — orange, lime green, black and her natural blonde-brown. Her face was thinner, harder looking. The lips had gone all the way from pouty to sullen.

"You let her walk around looking like this?"

"We knew — we thought it was just a phase she was going through. All kids do it."

"I suppose."

Maybe it wasn't all that different from the long-haired hippie look he'd worn as a teenager. What was probably bothering him more than the girl's looks, Swann realized, was his own reaction to it. He'd turned thirty-four earlier this year, but had only just started to become aware of that old age gap rearing its ugly head. Kids today just looked too weird for him and he was uncomfortable around them — something, when he was their age, he'd promised himself he'd never feel.

"What about her friends?" he asked. "Did any of them give you any leads on where she might have gone? Or why?"

"It turned out she really didn't have any friends. We never knew. We just — we just assumed she did. The agency we hired in Toronto could only find a couple of those punks that hang around on Yonge Street that knew her. All they could say was that she'd left town."

Swann gathered the photos and postcard together and tapped them against the table. "I don't know," he said. He laid them down and took a sip of his coffee. Belle showed up with a fried egg sandwich for him. He thanked her and took a big bite, using the time to try to come to a decision. Menzies' problem didn't look good.

"Arthur said…"

"What did he say?" Swann asked when Menzies' voice trailed off.

"That you cared."

Swann sighed. Lovely. He'd helped Arthur Davies out of a tricky situation last year — another missing persons case, only it was Davies' mother who'd gone AWOL from the retirement home she was living in here in Ottawa.

"How do you know Arthur?" he asked.

"He works for the ad agency that my firm deals with. We were working late one night on a new campaign and it just, you know, came up."

Swann studied the two pictures again. Before and after. Only after what? Swann didn't think he wanted to find out.

"I can pay," Menzies said.

"I'm sure you can, but it's not that. I just don't like the idea of you wasting your money. When people don't want to be found, especially a kid…"

"But you'll take the case?"

Swann eyed him thoughtfully. The eagerness in Menzies' voice masked a quiet desperation. He wondered how much Menzies had already put out to the other agencies and to the police — in both money and emotions. It wasn't easy having someone sift through your life on top of the anxiety you already felt in a situation like this, but that was what it took.

You had to know where the kid was coming from before you could work out where she'd gone.

"I'll do a little checking around," he said finally. "I can't promise you anything, but I'll touch base with one or two sources. If the case looks like it's going to lead back to Toronto, though, you might want to hire somebody local again. I can give you a couple of names if that happens."

Menzies looked grateful. He took an envelope from the same pocket that had given up the postcard and photos and handed it to Swann.

"This is a little extravagant," Swann said as he took a cheque for twelve hundred dollars out of the envelope. "Especially considering that I haven't really taken on the case."

"Arthur said you'd only take it on in a roundabout way."

I walked right into that one, Swann thought. He always did.

"What's the rest of this stuff?" he asked.

"It's the report from the Toronto agency." Menzies got up from the table as though he wanted to get away as quickly as he could before Swann changed his mind. "Thank you, Mr. Swann. You'll phone as soon as you have any word?"

Swann nodded and watched him go. He stuffed the cheque, photos and postcard into the envelope and stowed it all away in the side pocket of his sport jacket, then gave his attention to his rapidly-cooling sandwich. He still had another fifteen minutes until his next appointment, so he got up and borrowed Belle's newspaper and returned with it to his booth. He finished the sandwich, another coffee, and was just going through the third section of the paper, still looking for the funnies, when his next client almost bounced into the restaurant and sat down in his booth.

"It worked!" Roddy Brown said happily. "You put the fear of God into him, Mr. Swann. I doubt he'll even think about drugs anymore, little say try to deal them."

"Is that what he said?"

Roddy nodded. "I can't tell you how relieved I am. It had gotten to the point where every time I came home I expected to find that he'd been arrested. My nerves had nerves."

"But everything's okay now?"

"Perfect. And it can only get better."

Swann wasn't so sure about that, but he didn't feel like arguing the point. They'd already been through it all before. He took the roll of hundreds out of his pocket, peeled off two of them, and handed the remainder to Roddy.

"Two bills," he said. "That was the deal." And he had to have been crazy to make it in the first place, but what the hell. It was done now.

Roddy nodded. "Now I've got to find some way to get this back to him."

"Well, that's — if you don't mind me saying so — your problem. Just don't bring me into it, whatever you do. I could lose my license for just thinking of pulling off that kind of thing."

He didn't bother to mention that he knew Rocko and that it would take just a word in the right ear for Roddy and his friend Paul to be in more trouble than money could ever buy them out of. Swann hadn't really minded the deal, but he liked to cover his own ass.

"What did you do with the — you know?" Roddy asked.

"Flushed it."

"Oh. Well, I won't say a word to anyone, Mr. Swann. I can promise you that. Thanks again!"

He left the booth as cheerfully as he'd arrived and Swann just shook his head. Young love. Neither Roddy nor his roommate could be much over twenty.

Swann glanced at his watch and saw that he had a couple of hours to kill before he could start asking after the Menzies girl. The people he'd be asking didn't even think about getting up until around mid-afternoon. He reviewed his options. He could stay here and finish the paper, go back upstairs to his apartment and do a badly-needed laundry, or just go for a walk. Only the latter held any appeal.

It was a perfect day to hit the streets. The sun was shining and the sky so blue it hurt. Just the kind of day to take a leisurely stroll up along the canal to the Market. With any luck he'd run into Sammy Ward, playing her fiddle for quarters and dimes out in front of Zunder's Fruitland. He hadn't seen her since last Sunday when he'd bumped into her at a garage sale down in Sandy Hill. The little sod had snapped up a couple of books he'd had his eye on and then had the nerve to give them to him as a present.

He smiled, remembering. Paying his bill, he set off, hands in his pockets and humming a tune that Sammy always loved to play. Damned if he could remember its name. "The Humours of Something-or-other" was all he could come up with. He'd have to ask her what it was called if he did manage to run into her today.

T he day went sour.

Swann stared down at the sleeping figure in the hospital bed, his hands clenched into fists at his side. Sammy looked smaller than he remembered her to be. Her figure under the sheets went from slender to skinny in his mind. She was like a ghost of herself, hooked up to an IV, a bandage around her head, her face puffy and bruised. A swollen eye blinked open and regarded him from a circle of dark bruises.

"Hello, Jake. You got a smoke?"

Swann shook his head. He pulled a chair in from in front of the big window overlooking Smyth Road and sat down close to the head of the bed.

"No smoking in here, Sammy."

"It was worth a try."

She was trying to keep it light, but her voice was all wrong. Too tight. Hurting still, Swann thought. And not just from the physical pain.

"How'd you know I was in here?" she asked.

"I missed you in the Market. Then I ran into Toby and he told me."

"Word gets around."

"I guess." Swann looked away for a moment, glancing at the other beds in the ward. He leaned closer to her. "Who did it, Sammy?"

It was her turn to look away. "I don't know," she said, staring at the curtain dividing her part of the ward from the bed next to her. "But I know his face."

"Just one guy?"

She shook her head slightly. "But he was running the show."

"The cops been in to see you yet?"

"Yeah."

"What did you tell them?"

"Nothing."

Swann sighed. "Why not, Sammy? We can't let the bastards get away with this."

She turned to face him. "The guy that did this to me...he was a cop."

The day just got worse.

"How'd you know?" Swann asked. He was thinking of the little one-act performance he'd put on last night.

"He thought I was a hooker, Jake. He just wanted his cut of the action. I guess he takes it out of all the girls. When I wouldn't cooperate, he did...did all this to me. And then he and his friends had their...fun...anyway..."

Swann took her hand as gently as he could as she started to weep silently into her pillow. She flinched when he first touched her, then held tight, her face turned away from him. Swann sat like carved stone. His face was a mask. He wasn't sure how long he sat like that, holding her hand, being her lifeline to a world that wasn't filled with people who wanted to hurt her. It might have been a few minutes. It felt like forever.

When Sammy turned to face him again, her bruises were wet with tears.

"Get me out of here, Jake. Please."

"I'll talk to your doctor. If he says you've got to stay, can you hold out for a little longer?"

"I...I'll try."

"Soon as your doctor says it's okay, I'll spring you. You can stay in my spare room. I'll take care of you."

"Why are there people...people like him?"

"I don't know, Sammy. But I'm going to find out." He touched the back of his free hand gently against the side of her head. "Can you tell me anything about him—what he looked like, anything?"

"He was bigger than you, Jake. Just as tall, but bigger—you know? And he had a crewcut—salt-and-pepper hair."

"Anything else? A moustache maybe, or scars?"

Sammy lifted a trembling hand and touched the bottom of his chin. "He had a scar here—just a small one, like a triangle."

Swann saw her eyes welling up with tears again. Trying to describe the man just brought the memory of it back.

"Okay," he said. "That's enough for me to go on. You take it easy now."

"You're not going to leave?"

Swann shook his head. "Not till you're sleeping. And then I'll try to talk to your doctor. But don't be afraid of being here. Nobody's going to hurt you here. And I'll be back to see you tonight."

Her hand tightened on his. "You know, it's funny. After they dumped me from their car, all I could think about was that I'd never made it to the festival in Lisdoonvarna yet. I didn't even think about hurting or what they'd done to me...just that."

Lisdoonvarna. That was the name of the tune. Not "The Humours of Whatever," but "The Road to Lisdoonvarna."

"I was just thinking about that tune today," he said and hummed a few bars.

Sammy blinked, her eyes still shiny, but a faint smile touched her lips. "You never could hold a tune worth a shit," she said.

Swann grinned back. Let's pretend, he thought. Let's pretend that none of it happened. But it wasn't any good. He had a vague shape of a man sitting in the back of his head, just waiting for a face. There was going to be one unhappy cop in this city when Swann was through with him.

He sat there with her until she drifted off, then loosened her fingers from his and laid her hand on the bed. He stared down at it, remembering the music those fingers could call out of a fiddle, the way she could play tunes until you just had to smile. He hoped the music hadn't died in her.

———

"The doctor will be by later this afternoon," the head nurse told Swann. "I'll speak to him, but I don't think he'll let her go until Monday at the earliest. We're still waiting to run some tests, but this being the weekend..."

She shrugged and Swann felt like hitting something. It was unbelievable that most of a hospital could just shut down because it was the weekend.

"What're you saying?" he asked. "What kind of tests?"

"Well, we're afraid there might be internal injuries."

Jesus. Swann glanced at Sammy's bed. She still looked so small, lying there. The nurse regarded him sympathetically, but he could see behind her eyes that she'd been through this all a thousand times before.

"Okay," he said. "But ask the doctor for me anyway. I'll be back tonight. Any chance you could put her in a private room? I'll pay for it."

"I don't think there's anything free, but I'll check."

"Thanks. I'd appreciate that."

The nurse left him. He stood, studying Sammy for a few moments longer, then walked briskly from the room, heading for the elevators.

Five o Chapter

Swann took a cab from the hospital and had it drop him off in front of his Bank Street apartment. He went upstairs and checked in with his answering service. Sue told him there were no messages. He made a couple more phone calls, then put together a hospital care-package for Sammy — his Walkman with the rechargeable battery pack, some traditional music cassettes, a couple of books, and a nightshirt that would be too big for her, but would sure beat the open-backed gowns that they gave you in the hospital. He stowed it all away in an Adidas bag and left the apartment. When he reached his car, parked in an alley in back of his building, he threw the bag onto the back seat and coaxed the old Acadian into life. Ten minutes later he was pulling over to the curb in front of the five-story police station at Elgin and Catherine.

He turned on the radio and listened to the news on an AM station while he waited. Endless discussions on the new federal budget had been ousted by a cyclone in Bangladesh. After the news, Julian Lennon's "Valotte" came on and Detective-Inspector Lou Sweet was tapping at the window on the passenger's side. Swann leaned over and unlocked the door. Lou slipped in.

"Shit on wheels," he said. "When are you going to start driving something decent?"

"I don't get kickback—though I do just as much detecting as you. Soon as I can afford it, I'll get myself a nice Mercedes like you've probably got hidden away in your garage."

"Fun-nee."

"Want to go for a beer?"

"Sure."

Swann put the car into first and headed for the Driveway that would take them back into the Glebe where Swann lived. He liked to do his buying in his own neighbourhood when he could.

"Gives me the creeps," Lou said.

"What does?"

"Lennon's kid. Sounds just like his old man."

"I kind of like the fact that we've still got that voice around—or something so close it might as well be the same."

"I'll bet the kid would really like to hear that."

Swann shrugged. He'd hit puberty around the same time that the Beatles made it big. His first backseat romances and their music were inextricably entwined.

He parked the Acadian in front of the Brewers' Retail on Bank and they crossed the street to the R&R. Late on a Saturday afternoon, and with nothing on at Lansdowne Park down the street, there were just the usual regulars in the restaurant.

"That's what I like about you, Swann," Lou said as they took a window table. "I can always count on going someplace classy when I'm with you."

"Beats paying for it, though."

"There's that."

He ordered an Ex and a shot of whiskey. Swann settled on a Budweiser.

"So what's the occasion?" Lou asked after they'd been served.

"I'm trying to place one of your detectives—a guy in Morality, I'd guess. Same height as me, a little heavier. Salt-and-pepper crewcut. Triangular scar here, just under the chin. Ring any bells?"

"Sounds like Rankin — Bob Rankin. What do you want with him?"

The question was natural enough, but Swann could almost see the gears shift in Lou's mind as he tried to make a connection.

"I'm just running down a lead on a case I'm working on."

"This got anything to do with that friend of yours that got knocked around last night?"

Lou had a quick mind — too quick for Swann's liking. Especially when he was trying to run one by his friend. Lou Sweet was a career cop. He'd signed up right after graduating from high school and worked his way up through the ranks over the past twenty-two years to the position he had now. He was five-ten, a half head shorter than Swann, and bulky. He had the caricatured square jaw of a cop, short brown hair, thinning at the top, cool grey eyes. And he was smart. Tenacious as a snapping turtle when it got its jaws onto you and just as quick.

"How'd you hear about Sammy?" Swann asked.

Lou shrugged. "The report crossed my desk. I know who your friends are, Swann. So what's this got to do with Rankin?"

"Nothing. He works for Morality?"

When Lou nodded, Swann pulled the photos of Trish Menzies from his pocket and laid them on the table in front of his friend.

"Missing persons?" Lou asked.

"Yeah. Out of T.O. I thought if she blew into town, broke, she might end up down in the Market, turning tricks. Maybe dancing in a strip club."

"And Rankin?"

"Somebody said I should look him up, but they didn't have a name."

"Well, he works that area. You want me to set up a meet with him for you?"

Swann shook his head. "No. I can handle that. What's he like? Do you know him?"

"He's a name. I know his face to see him. He does a lot of liaison work—you know, when we're setting up investigations with the OPP or the Horsemen."

"I thought you said he was in Morality."

"The immoral know no boundaries," Lou said with a grin. "Unlike jurisdictions. We going for another round?"

"Sure." Swann signaled the waitress.

"Listen," Lou said. "I'm sorry about Sammy. Really. It's a fucking shame that kind of shit goes on. And it's just getting worse. I got ten times the reports crossing my desk now than there were when I first made detective."

"Yeah," Swann said. "I know."

"Your friend didn't get a make on the guys that jumped her."

It was a statement, rather than a question, but Swann shook his head. "I think she just blocked it out."

"Are you planning to look into it?"

"I've got nothing to go on."

Swann looked up to see how Lou took the lie. He couldn't read anything in those grey poker eyes.

"Well, if you do get anything," Lou said finally, "don't go playing lone wolf. Call me."

"I'm not one of your men," Swann said. "I'm private— remember?"

"Yeah. But you're a friend."

"That counts," Swann said. He gathered up the photos and returned them to their envelope. The waitress brought their second round and he paid her with a twenty.

"It counts for me, too," Lou said. "So call me—okay?"

Swann nodded. "Sure. But I've already got a case."

Swann returned to the General Hospital at seven. He parked on Linda Lane to save himself the parking fee in the hospital's lot and walked across a narrow band of greenery and the doctors' parking lot to get to the front door, swinging his Adidas bag in his left hand. He took the elevator up to the sixth floor, feeling nervous. Hospitals did that to him. All the sterility of their halls and wards couldn't hide the fact that illness was trapped in them. He could feel it, waiting in the walls like Legionnaire's disease, ready to grab him.

Sammy was still in a four-bed ward. They hadn't moved her. She was sleeping and didn't look any better to Swann's layman's eye. Jimmy Crackle was sitting in the chair that Swann had vacated earlier.

He was a full-blooded Ojibwa, thin as a sapling and wiry. There was a touch of grey in his blue-black braids and his deep brown eyes held a world-weary look. His copper skin was a complex roadmap of wrinkles. Swann didn't know how old he was. He'd known Jimmy for the better part of two decades and all he knew of him was what they'd experienced together. Nothing of his past. Nothing of what he did when he wasn't around Swann.

"Hey, Jimmy. Thanks for coming." He leaned over the bed to peer closer at Sammy. "How's she doing?"

"No change."

"Has the doctor been by to see her?"

Jimmy Crackle nodded. "He said she's stuck here till Monday—that's the earliest he'll let her out, depending on the tests."

"Any other visitors?"

"Not since I've been here. What's up, Jevon?"

Swann gave him a brief rundown. "She doesn't know if she can recognize any of the others," he finished.

"So what's next?"

"Well, I was hoping to take her home with me. I don't think she should be alone here, but I've got some things that need doing tonight."

"I can stay with her."

"That's awfully white of you."

Jimmy Crackle grinned. Sammy woke before he could frame a suitable reply.

"Jake?" she asked softly from the bed.

"I'm here, Sammy. I brought you some stuff to make the time go faster." He laid the Adidas bag on the bed and zipped it open.

"Just so long as it goes," Sammy said.

Her voice still wasn't any good, Swann thought. His knuckles whitened around the handle of the bag. He took a slow breath and let it out, forcing himself to stay calm. But it was hard. Looking at her, at what they did to her, hearing her voice, so…empty when it was always full of life…

Jimmy Crackle stood up and pulled a moosehide tobacco pouch from his shirt pocket. "I'm going down the hall for a smoke, Jevon. Call me when you're leaving."

Swann nodded. He waited until Jimmy had left the ward, then sat down in the chair by the head of the bed. He stayed there for awhile, holding her hand, then he started taking the tapes and books out of the bag.

"Here," he said. "This is the new Phil Cunningham LP. It's got some hot tunes on it. And this one's by George Jackson—

one of the Ossian boys — and somebody called Maggie MacInnes. A harper. Did you ever hear of her?"

"Not so's I remember."

"Wait'll you hear the title cut — 'Cairistiona.' It'll knock your socks off. Or maybe not. I guess the nurses already took your socks, right?

Sammy tried to smile.

"You want I should order you a TV? I'm trying for a private room but they're not exactly falling over themselves to get one for you."

"I don't need a TV," she said. "I just need there to be someone in here with me. Someone I know. Someone I can trust."

Swann nodded. "I've got some work to do tonight, but Jimmy'll stay on. Is that okay?"

"They'll make him go at eight-thirty — that's when visiting hours are over."

"No one makes Jimmy go if he doesn't want to."

"That's good. I...I just don't want to be alone."

She took his hand again and squeezed it hard. Swann's throat tightened with emotion. Cop or no cop, Bob Rankin was going to be one sorry bastard when Swann was through with him.

"Did I tell you I had a gig in a couple of weeks?"

Swann shook his head.

"Yeah. Me and Wes Thompson. It was going to be on the outdoor patio at The Earl."

"There'll be other gigs, Sammy."

"I guess."

"There will be."

"Will you tell Wes for me? Tell him what — " She broke off, cleared her throat. "Just tell him that I won't be able to make it. He's working that little tunnel across the street from the Chateau, most weekdays around noon. He'll have either a guitar or a bouzouki — maybe both."

"I'll tell him."

She let go of his hand and looked at a couple of the tapes. When Swann made a cassette, he usually cut pictures out of magazines and inserted them in the casings, rather than listing the titles of the songs. The one Sammy was looking at was out of a magazine called *Ireland of the Welcomes,* an Irish craft magazine. It showed an old couple standing in front of a crofter's cottage in the Aran Islands.

Sammy laid the tape down on the swinging table beside the bed. Her eyes welled with tears.

"What am I going to do, Jake?" she asked in a low voice. "I don't feel like I'll be safe anywhere anymore. All I was doing was coming home after a run when they...they..."

"No one's going to hurt you again," Swann said. "I promise that."

She reached for a tissue, but her IV held her arm back. Swann got it for her. She dabbed it around her eyes, careful of the bruises.

"Can you find him for me, Jake?" she asked.

"Who?"

"The bastard who did this to me. All of them, but especially the guy who was in charge."

"That's a job for the cops, Sammy."

"He *was* a cop. Please, Jake. Can't you do something? I've heard all the talk on the streets. Everybody knows that you...stretch the rules a little. You and Bo."

"Right. And we'd be the first people they'd come looking for. They'd just love to put us away, Sammy. Do you want that?"

"No. It's just...I don't want him to get away with what he did. I want him to hurt as much as I did. As I do. Can't you understand that?"

"Sure. But what's it going to get you? It might seem trite, but revenge never really satisfies, Sammy. That guy'll get his."

"I want to *see* him get his," she said fiercely. "I want to see him begging like he had me doing and then have it happen to him anyway. I want him to die *knowing* why."

You and me both, Swann thought. But there was no way he was going to let Sammy get involved, no matter how he finally decided to deal with Rankin. She could get her satisfaction knowing that he'd got what was coming to him, but she wasn't going to know who did it. And she wasn't going to be there.

"Can...can't I hire you or something?" Sammy asked.

"I've already got a case," Swann said. "And I don't kill guys for money."

Sammy just stared at him. Slowly what he'd said sank in. "Oh, jeez," she said softly. "I wasn't really...I didn't mean..."

"I know, Sammy. It hurts and you want to hurt him back, but you're not really that kind of person. That just takes you down to his level and you don't want to know about that kind of place. A guy like him'll get his without you doing anything about it."

Sammy nodded. "I just feel...I feel like trash, Jake. Like I'm finished and it's time to throw old Sammy Ward away."

He held her hand again and stroked her temple with gentle fingers. "Things'll change. Maybe what you're feeling now won't ever go completely away, but it'll fade. The sharp edges'll wear down a little. Nature put together a great mechanism when it designed us, Sammy. We can roll with punches like you wouldn't believe."

"Even this?" she asked in a small voice.

"Even this," Swann assured her. "But it's going to take some time."

"I don't know if I've got that kind of time."

"I'll help you, Sammy. That's what friends are for."

The announcement that visiting hours were over came over the intercom—first in French, then in English. Jimmy Crackle appeared at the door of the ward and wandered over to Sammy's bed.

"Have you two met?" Swann asked.

"This afternoon. I was awake when he came in. The first thing he said was, 'Jevon Swann asked me to come sit with

you, only he never told me you were going to be so pretty.'"
Sammy looked at Swann. "Did you think I was pretty,
before...you know?"

"Still do," Swann said. "Though I'm not big on your
makeup."

Sammy lifted a hand to her face. "So how came you never
made a pass at me?"

"Didn't think you'd be interested in an old coot like me
and I didn't want to chase you off by trying."

"You're a funny guy, Jake."

"All my friends say that. If it keeps up, I might get a
complex."

"Just don't change."

"No worry of that happening," Jimmy Crackle said. "Did
you ever see his car? A man that'd drive a machine like that is
just too set in his ways to change."

"I've got to run," Swann said. "Are you going to be okay?"

Sammy nodded.

"Okay. I'll be by later tonight."

"They won't let you in."

"We'll see." Swann turned to Jimmy Crackle. "Nobody
comes near her without her okay."

"I think I can handle that."

"Thanks, Jimmy."

"Keep a back door open," Jimmy Crackle said.

"I'll do that."

He brushed the top of Sammy's head with his lips and left
just as the nurse came in to tell them that they had to leave.
He didn't stick around to see how she dealt with the
immovable force that Jimmy Crackle could be. It was enough
to know that Jimmy would be there.

Swann parked his Acadian in an alley behind the old
police station on Waller Street. The city was now using the
building for emergency housing. He locked the car, then went
in search of a phone booth. There were over thirty Rankins in
the city directory, but only one Robert. Swann studied the
listing. Rankin lived on Bathurst. He thought for a moment,
then placed it. Riverview Park. South of the Main Post Office
on Industrial.

He didn't bother trying to memorize the listing. He'd
always had a lousy memory. Instead he simply ripped the page
out of the directory. And he wondered why Bell Canada's
phone rates were so high.

Folding the page, he added it to the growing inventory of
papers in the inner pocket of his sport jacket. He was starting
to feel like the file drawer he'd told Menzies he didn't believe
in. A quick glance up and down Rideau Street, then he headed
north for the Market area. It took him twenty minutes to finally
run down Happy Cohen.

He found him sitting on the Earl of Sussex's outdoor patio,
right across the street from where the ambulance had picked
up Sammy last night. If things had worked out differently, she'd
be playing here in a week or so.

"Hey, Cohen," he said, sliding into a vacant chair across
from him. "Looks like you're feeling flush."

Happy Cohen had three draft beers lined up in front of him—two full, one half empty. He lived on the street, but was cleaner than the average itinerant. He had a bony frame and potbelly that made him look like a famine victim but he was always smiling. He drank, but he never got drunk. His hair was longish and always looked like he only used his fingers to comb it. His jeans were worn and patched, his T-shirt new. It said "Twisted Sister" above a crude drawing of the leering features of the band's blonde lead singer. Swann wondered if Cohen had ever heard what the band sounded like. In his late forties, Cohen was hardly a part of the generation that went in for heavy metal music.

"You know how it goes, Swann," he said. "Comes and goes." He pushed one of the full drafts across the table to Swann.

"Thanks. I've got a picture I want you to have a look at. Are you working?"

"I'm always working, Swann. How much?"

"A twenty—if the information's good."

"Like you said, Swann. I'm feeling flush. Is this something long term as in, can I get back to you with it?"

"Twenty now, another twenty if you come up with something."

What the hell, Swann thought. It wasn't his money. Menzies could afford it.

"Another forty," Cohen said.

Swann smiled. "I hate it when you're flush." He handed over a twenty along with the two pictures.

Happy Cohen took a long swig of his draft, finishing it off. He set the mug aside and pulled the other one over until it was centered exactly in front of him. Then he studied the pictures.

"I've seen her," he said.

"Recently?"

"Yeah. But I can't remember where."

"Another forty's all you're getting—tops."

Happy Cohen shook his head. "I'm not trying to up the ante. I just can't remember. I've got to ask around. You need these?"

"They're all I've got."

"Give me ten minutes," Cohen said.

When Swann nodded, he gathered up the photos and headed across the street. He went into the little park, then was lost to view. Swann looked away. Rankin. That's where he'd dumped Sammy.

Cohen was gone just two minutes past his deadline. Swann had finished his beer and ordered another for both of them. Cohen smiled when he saw the fresh draft sitting beside the one he'd left and dropped the photos on Swann's side of the table.

"You get them copied?"

Cohen nodded.

"Where'd you get them done?"

"You don't need to know, Swann. That's all. I got a friend with a photocopier."

"Handy to know — if I ever need copies late on a Saturday night."

"You just come see me, Swann. I'm always open for business with you."

Swann gathered up the photos and tucked them back into his pocket. "You still got my number?" he asked.

"Depends. Sue Wheeler still working your answering service?"

Swann nodded.

"Then I've still got your number. I'll call you soon. Maybe tomorrow."

"I appreciate it," Swann said. He stood up and dropped a five on the table to cover the beers.

"You didn't finish yours," Cohen said.

"I've got work to do. You finish it for me. Thanks for the brew, Cohen."

"I'll be in touch."

Swann nodded and headed back up Sussex to where he'd left his car. He'd just covered his ass in case Lou asked around and wondered why he wasn't making an effort to chase down the Menzies girl. It also took a small chunk out of the cheque Menzies had given him. He'd keep at it. But first he had some unfinished business with a cop named Rankin.

Chapter Eight

Bathurst ran southeast between Mimosa and Chadburn, with a slight curve at its lower end where it hit Chadburn. Swann cruised slowly by Rankin's house, noted the two cars in the lane—a dark green Mazda and an old Plymouth—and drove on by. He parked on Chadburn and walked back. It was just going on eleven.

Now that he was walking the area, he remembered it from when he was a kid. He'd been going out with a girl who'd lived on Devon Street. Gloria Boyer. Glory-o, he used to call her. Her parents' house backed onto Balena Park.

Swann stood at the beginning of the park now. Rankin's house looked over the wide green field. The two baseball diamonds were still there. A strip of forest lay beyond the field. A hydro line followed the northwest side of the park, the tall dress-form shapes marching into the trees in a straight southwesterly line, crossing Smyth Road and proceeding on into the far distance. Soldiers in the war to provide ever more electricity to the city, Swann thought. We stand on guard for thee.

His gaze left them and centered on the lights of the General Hospital that could be seen above the trees from where he stood. He counted down until he had the sixth floor.

Sammy.

Rankin.

He crossed the street and moved onto the lawn that separated Rankin's house from his eastern neighbour's.

He didn't have a plan just yet. First he wanted to put a face to the featureless figure standing in the back of his head. He also wanted to be absolutely sure he had the right man. That wasn't going to be as easy.

There was no one in the living room, so he sidled towards the back of the house. He should have asked Lou if Rankin had a dog. If he was married. How many kids he had. There were a lot of things he could have asked Lou. Like, so what do you think, Lou? Bob Rankin the kind of guy that'd brutally rape a nice kid like Sammy? He decided he'd rather find his own answers.

Light spilled from the kitchen into the backyard, falling on a small patio. There were a couple of lawn chairs, a cedar picnic table, a gas barbecue. All the comforts. The shadowy shape of a metal toolshed stood at the back of the yard. You got an axe in there, Rankin? Swann thought. Some garden shears maybe? He was feeling violent. Every time he thought of *why* he was here, his chest felt like it was in a vise.

He moved to the closest window. Be just his luck, some neighbour would spy him and call the cops. He peered in and saw three men sitting around the kitchen table, talking, laughing, putting back a few cold ones. A typical Saturday night suburban scene. The man with his back to the window was broad-shouldered, his hair salt and pepper. Rankin. Across from him was a man who seemed vaguely familiar to Swann, but he couldn't place him. He was dressed in a tennis shirt and pressed cotton trousers. Neat short hair, parted on the left. Strong jaw, Roman nose.

The third man was Lou Sweet.

Swann turned away from the window and sank slowly against the wall. Lou. Wasn't that a pisser?

He's a name. I know his face to see him.

Well, I guess you do, Lou. I just guess you fucking do.

It took all his will to control the rage building up inside him. He breathed slowly, long deep breaths, until the anger subsided into a dull ache. He waited until he was sure he had himself under control before moving down along the back of the house. He still needed a face to go with Rankin's name. And a name to go with the third man's face. Standing on the back steps and looking in, he could see Rankin in profile. That was enough. He backed down the steps and circled around to the front of the house.

The Plymouth was Lou's. Swann had ridden around in it often enough, but it was a nondescript vehicle and he hadn't even stopped to consider he might know it. Checking the garage, he spied a shiny Corvette sitting inside. So odds were the Mazda belonged to the third man. He moved towards it, looked up and down the street quickly, then tried the door. Locked on the driver's side. No reason to suppose it would be any different on the passenger's.

He took a small leather case from his pocket and selected a pair of lockpicks from it. Crouching down beside the car, he worked them inside and popped the lock in just under thirty seconds. Stowing the picks away, he opened the door and slipped inside. The glove compartment was unlocked, but there was nothing in it that gave any clue as to the car's owner. Maps. An Owner's Manual. A hodgepodge collection of fast food napkins and pouches of salt, pepper, sugar, ketchup, vinegar and mustard. Real big spender. There was also a pen.

It was the same story under the seats and in the back. Okay, Swann thought. So it's not going to be easy. He left the car, keeping the pen. Locking the door behind him, he dragged Menzies' envelope out and copied the Mazda's plate number down on it. Sticking the envelope and pen in his pocket, he started back for his car. He'd learned all he could for now. It was time to get back to the hospital.

It was a five minute walk from Rankin's to the General Hospital, straight across fields and a thin strip of forest. Going by car, Swann had to backtrack to Alta Vista Drive and then take the long way around. He left the Acadian by the front doors of the hospital and took the stairs up to the sixth floor. He reached Sammy's ward without being stopped by one of the night nurses. Jimmy Crackle looked up from his chair and crossed the room.

"How's she doing?" Swann asked softly as he backed into the hall.

Jimmy Crackle shrugged. "You look like shit, Jevon."

"It's not been my favorite day."

He filled Jimmy in on his night, not keeping anything back.

"Go home and get some sleep, Jevon," Jimmy Crackle said. "I'm okay here."

"You've got things to do, I'm sure. Thanks, but—"

"Sitting here's what I've got to do tonight, Jevon. Come back in the morning when you look a little more human."

"I'll just look in on her."

"Sure. I wanted a smoke anyway."

Swann stood over Sammy's bed and looked down at her sleeping features. There was little light in the room—only what spilled in from the hallway. She looked more herself in the dim lighting. Still puffy, but the bruising just looked like shadows now.

"There's a nurse coming," Jimmy Crackle said quietly. "You'd better go."

Swann started. He'd lost all track of time just standing there and never even heard Jimmy approach.

"Okay," he said.

Jimmy Crackle touched his arm as he started to go. "Don't start anything, Jevon. Not without calling in some backup. Give Bo a call."

"What's to start?" Swann asked.

"I know you. Just keep a lid on it."

"Sure."

"Excuse me," a woman's voice said from the door. "But you can't—"

"This is Jean," Jimmy Crackle said. "She's taking care of Sammy tonight."

Swann turned to look at the nurse. She was short and plump in her starched whites. Smile lines creased her face, but she wasn't smiling now.

"Keep up the good work," Swann said as he brushed by her.

"You can't just—"

"Say," Jimmy Crackle said. "I think this woman's IV's come loose."

"What?"

"Maybe I was mistaken."

Swann had found the exit to the stairs and closed the door behind him, cutting off the rest of their conversation. He padded lightly down the stairs. He was still too wound up—Lou's defection hurt almost as much as it did to look at Sammy's bruises. Ten years they'd been friends. And now this. Like a knife in the back.

He drove home too fast.

There were two of them waiting for him in the alley behind his apartment where he parked his car. He spotted them as he got out of the Acadian, but it was too late to retreat. They were big — each of them at least his size. He didn't figure they were here to invite him to a party.

He waited until they were just a few yards away, then moved quickly towards them. There was nothing threatening about the way he approached. He had both hands up in the air at chest level, as though to hold them back.

"Hey, guys," he said. "Can't we just talk?"

He could feel them relax. That was when he stepped in close and hit the first man. He didn't draw back his arm, just jabbed him hard, two lightning blows that struck the man just below the sternum. He dropped like a felled log. Swann turned to the second man who had taken a half-step back.

"You ever see *Billy Jack?*" Swann asked.

"What?"

"You know — the bit about watch my foot hit your head?"

The second man came at him then and Swann bunched his leg muscles and jumped. He kicked the second man in the head and dislocated his jaw. He also ripped the seat out of his own pants.

"Shit," he muttered. How come that never happened to Chuck Norris?

He crouched beside the man and hit him quickly with the side of his hand, silencing him. Then he moved to the first man he'd taken out.

"Who sent you?" he demanded.

The man wheezed, fighting for air. Swann repeated the question. When he got no reply, he squeezed a nerve in the man's neck and he joined his partner in slumberland. Swann went through the man's pockets. He found a wallet in the back left hand pocket of his pants, but the name on the driver's license didn't mean anything to him. At least they weren't cops. From their size, and considering what he was getting himself into, Swann had been half-expecting them to be police.

He took the second man's wallet as well and found he was carrying a handgun. A .357 Magnum in a shoulder holster. Swann lifted it free and studied it for a moment. He could use this, but it would be just asking for trouble. If Lou or Rankin decided to pick him up or give his place a tumble, it was just the kind of thing they could use against him.

He threw the wallets into a garbage dumpster farther down the alley, then wrapped the Magnum in a discarded plastic bag and stashed it under some debris by the fire escape that led up to his apartment. The two men he dragged out to the mouth of the alleyway, then he phoned in an anonymous tip to the police. He was standing on his fire escape, sipping a Budweiser, when the police car came for them. He drifted back into his apartment as one of the officers came down the alley with a flashlight. Closing his backdoor silently, Swann went looking for a clean, untorn pair of jeans, then decided against it. He was just planning to hit the sack anyway.

He threw the torn pants in a corner and sat down on the bed in his boxer shorts. Pulling the phone over to him, he hooked the receiver under his ear and dialed his answering service. Sue answered on the second ring.

"Hi, Sue. Didn't get you up, did I?"

"No. I was just watching the late movie. There's a couple of messages here for you."

"Shoot."

"Mr. Menzies called and he wants you to call back. Before eleven tonight—I guess it's too late for that—or tomorrow morning before twelve."

Swann made a note on his Post-it pad as she spoke, tore it free and stuck it on the wall beside his bed. "What about the other one?"

"Lou called. He wants you to get back to him tonight—doesn't matter what time you get in."

Swann frowned. "Okay. Thanks, Sue. What's the movie you're watching?"

"_Purple Rain._ They're finally running it on First Choice. It's just started."

Swann had met Sue Wheeler through a case he'd been working on a few years ago. She was a plain-looking woman, bordering on plump, except for her legs which were as thin as a pair of rake handles. She had been in a car accident the year before Swann met her that had paralyzed her from the waist down. The other driver's insurance company managed to pull a fast one and all Sue ever got out of them was her medical expenses. By the time her appeal went to court, the firm had gone bankrupt. It had been Swann's idea to set her up in the answering service business. She had about twenty clients now.

"Want me to tell you how it ends?" Swann asked.

"I _know_ how it ends. I just want to see Prince strut his stuff. What time do you want your wake-up call tomorrow?"

"Sevenish."

"Are you serious?"

"I'm a busy man, Sue." He thought about the two men he'd left for the police. "Everybody wants a piece of me these days. Talk to you tomorrow, okay? And enjoy the movie."

"I will. Goodnight, Jake."

Swann cradled the receiver, then stared at the phone for a long moment. He got up and dropped his empty beer can in the kitchen garbage and fetched a fresh Bud from the fridge. Peering out the window, he could see the red lights of an ambulance flickering in the alley below. They were loading a stretcher as he returned to his bedroom and dialed Lou Sweet's number.

"Swann here," he said when Lou answered.

"Where've you been, Swann? A hot and heavy date? Oh, shit. I'm sorry. I forgot about Sammy."

Sure you did, Swann thought. Were you one of the guys with Rankin that night, Lou?

"Sue said you wanted to talk to me," he said into the phone.

"Yeah. It's about Rankin."

"What about him?"

"Have you talked to him yet?"

"No. I'm running down a couple of other leads first. Why?"

"Well, it might be a good idea if you stayed away from him, Swann."

"Says who?"

"Don't get your back up, Swann."

"My back's not up. I'm just curious. What's so special about Rankin?"

"Between you and me?"

"Sure."

"We're running an investigation on him."

"I thought you said you didn't know him."

"I don't. Not socially. But this thing going down with Rankin could get messy. It's touch and go now and we don't know how deep it's going. I got to thinking after you dropped me off tonight. I'd hate to see you get caught up in it. The Chief's got no reason to love you as it is."

"I'm just looking for a girl, Lou. I don't need him to find her, do I?"

"I hope not."

"Just what's he being investigated for anyway?"

"I can't tell you that, Swann."

"Sure. Well, thanks for the tip."

"We've got to look out for our friends, right? I'll talk to you later, Swann."

"Yeah. Goodnight, Lou."

And fuck you, you lying bastard.

Swann forced himself to set the receiver gently in its cradle instead of smashing it down. Sure Lou didn't know Bob Rankin.

Not socially.

Swann drained his beer, then crushed the can in his fist and threw it at the wall.

The lying sonuvabitch.

Seven-fifteen, Sunday morning, Swann took a perverse pleasure in calling Walter Menzies. He figured if he had to be up at this ungodly hour, everybody else might as well be up, too. It was a variation on the old the world-ends-when-I-go syndrome. Childish, but these days his life held too few smiles.

Menzies sounded depressingly alert when he came on the line.

"Hello? Mr. Swann?"

"I'm here. You left a message?"

"Is there any news?"

Most people were like that. You took on their case and they expected results yesterday.

"I'm still working on it. The earliest I'll know anything is tonight. I'll get back to you as soon as there's something to tell you, Mr. Menzies."

"Yes. Of course. It's just that I've begun to hope again and…" His voice trailed off. "I'll wait for your call."

"And I'll do the best I can," Swann told him before he cut the connection.

He spent the rest of the day in the hospital with Sammy, after first having a word aside with Jimmy Crackle to fill him in on last night's attack.

"I'll give Bo a call," Jimmy said. "This a paying job?"

Swann shook his head. "Not if it's connected with what happened to Sammy. I can't see it being tied to the Menzies girl. But I've got money."

"That won't matter to Bo. Doesn't matter to me, either. If you're doing a freebie, we'll do it at the same rate you're getting. What time do you want me to get back here? Eight — eight-thirty?"

"Thanks, Jimmy."

"Means you owe me a fishing trip."

Swann laughed. "You've got it."

He went in to sit with Sammy after Jimmy Crackle left. The hospital had finally given up a private room. It was in the southwest corner of the sixth floor and commanded a good view of Rideau Park and the fields southeast of it through a wall-sized picture window that started around mid-thigh on Swann and went on up to the ceiling. Rideau Park looked more like a forest than a subdivision from this height. Only the odd upper story or roof of a house could be seen through the green blanketed cover.

Swann had brought a cribbage board and a pack of cards with him today. He and Sammy spent the day just talking, playing crib, and trying to puzzle out what the meals were supposed to be as opposed to what they looked and tasted like. Sometimes they just sat in that companionable quiet that they'd shared from the first time they'd gotten to know each other. All the day missed was the traditional music on the stereo that played almost constantly in both their apartments. Swann's Walkman only had one set of headphones.

Sammy's doctor came by in the afternoon and gave her a look over while Swann waited in the hall. Afterwards, the doctor called him in.

"Your breathing sounds better," the doctor told Sammy, "and I'm pretty sure we can let you go home tomorrow, but I'd still like to take some X-rays in the morning."

Sammy glanced at Swann.

"Might as well," he said. He knew she wanted out, but why take chances?

"I'll see you tomorrow then," the doctor said. "After the X-rays."

"I feel like I'm going to be here forever," Sammy said after the doctor left, "but the funny thing is I don't really mind anymore. I feel safe here now — with you and Jimmy watching over me."

"You're just going to keep getting better," Swann told her.

"I don't like feeling this scared. I feel that if I'm alone, it's going to happen again."

Swann shook her head. "I won't let it happen again, Sammy."

He didn't bother to explain how he'd manage that and she didn't ask. For the moment it was enough that the words were said.

Jimmy Crackle returned at twenty past eight.

"I've got some business to take care of again," Swann said. "Will you be okay with Jimmy?"

"Sure. Thanks, Jake."

Swann was glad to leave her in better spirits than she'd felt since he first came in yesterday afternoon. Her bruises seemed darker — a sign that they were healing, according to the nurse. Sammy still looked rough. She still sounded bad. But she was healing.

He checked in with Sue on one of the pay phones downstairs and found that there was a message for him from Happy Cohen. He called the number Sue gave him.

"You want to see a guy called Skiv," Happy Cohen said. "He's going to be at a party on Cooper Street for the rest of the night."

Cohen gave him the house number.

"What's he look like?"

"Orange Mohawk — you can't miss him. Of course, that depends on what the rest of the crowd's like. Just ask for him at the door. He's expecting you."

"How much'll he want?"

"You'll have to negotiate that with him yourself, Swann. If it works out, you can catch me on the Mall tomorrow afternoon."

"I'll have your money then."

"I hope it works out," Happy Cohen said. "I'm not feeling so flush today."

It was dark by the time Swann left the hospital and walked to where he'd left his car. He'd parked on Smyth this time. The air felt good after a day in the sterile environment of the hospital. He was looking forward to taking Sammy out of the place.

He got into the Acadian and coaxed it to start one more time, then pulled out into the light Sunday evening traffic. It wasn't until he was on Main Street, turning left on Riverdale, that he spotted the dark brown Buick on his tail.

Chapter Twelve

Bo Jeffries was waiting for Swann in Swann's apartment. Swann didn't bother to ask how he'd gotten in. Everything Swann knew about picking locks and illegal entry he'd learned from Bo. Unlike Bo, he'd never done time for utilizing those particular skills.

Bo was like a small mountain sitting in Swann's favorite chair. He had a thatch of dark brown hair and a muscle-builder's physique. Weighing in at two-fifty, he stood six-three and always filled a room. His eyes were small in a broad field of a face. On the knuckles of each hand were reminders of the time he'd done in prison. The right hand said "love," the left "hate," in the faded blue-black that was the result of tattoos made with nothing more than ink and a pin. There was another on his shoulder, hidden now by the sleeve of his black T-shirt, of a knife blade dripping a drop of blue-black blood.

Lying at Bo's feet was a fat white bull terrier that jumped to its feet and raced across the room to meet Swann, thrusting its muzzle up towards his crotch. The dog always reminded Swann of a little white pig with a black pirate's patch over its left eye. With typical insight, Bo had named it Sooey.

"Want a beer?" Bo asked. "I think there's one left."

Swann eyed the five empty cans lined neatly on the coffee table in front of Bo. "Been here long?" he asked.

"A couple of hours. The Indian called—said you might need a hand."

"Yeah. Did he tell you about it?"

"Said you'd fill me in."

Swann went into the kitchen to get his last beer before it disappeared down Bo's throat and returned to the living room, Sooey at his heels. Sitting down across from Bo, he proceeded to outline the past few days.

"Picked up a tail coming back from the hospital," he said as he finished.

"Did you lose it?"

"Why bother? I was coming home and I figured they'd know where I live."

Bo nodded. He finished off his last beer and lined the empty can up beside the other five.

"I don't figure Sweet being in on this," he said.

"I saw him at Rankin's—just as happy as you please." "It's just hard to believe. I mean, I've been ragging on him for years—but it was always just a joke, right? I always figured Sweet to be about as straight as they come."

"Yeah. So did I."

Bo sighed. He looked over to the door leading into the kitchen as though he hoped that the fridge might have spontaneously regenerated some more beer, then settled more deeply in his seat. The chair gave an ominous moan.

"What's the story with Sammy? You never told me you were getting serious with her."

"All she knows is street people," Swann said, "and they can't exactly provide the stability and shelter she's got to have right now. I figure she needed someone, that's all."

"You sound to me like it's running a little deeper'n that."

"You know me and women—it never works out. I like what I've got with Sammy. I don't want to screw it up by getting all hot and heavy with her."

Bo shook his head. "You're some kinda weird shit, you know that, Jake? Sounds to me like she's just what you need."

"She's got to be ten years younger than me."

"Oh—I get it. You're too mature for her, is that it?"

"Let's just drop it, okay?"

"Sure. So what do you want me to do?"

"You still got that friend at the Ministry of Transport?"

When Bo nodded, Swann tugged open his file-drawer pocket and took out the envelope and the pen he'd lifted from the Mazda. Tearing off a strip of paper from the bottom of the agency report that Menzies had given him, he copied the license plate number of the Mazda down and handed it to Bo.

"This the car that was out at Rankin's?" Bo asked.

"Yeah. Can you find out who it's registered to?"

"No problem. Anything else?"

Swann shook his head. "I've got to take a run over to Cooper Street and talk to this Skiv still."

"Man on the run," Bo said. "You gonna finish that beer?"

"What do you think?"

Bo grinned. "Just asking."

Swann tipped the can back and drained it.

"One more thing," Bo said. "I got a call from BB&R. They've got a job for me—insurance fraud—only thing is I need your name on the contract. They just love paperwork. Any problem with that?"

Swann shook his head. "You want a hand with it?"

"Naw. It's a piece of cake. I'll give you your usual commission."

Private investigators in the province of Ontario were licensed by the Ontario Provincial Police. The OPP refused to give Bo an okay because of his record so he used Swann's name to get jobs where a piece of paper needed to be signed. They were partners of a sort, though Swann just listed Bo as casual labour when he filed his income tax.

"You want to do something about your tail?" Bo asked as Swann got up. "I could maybe, you know, convince 'em to take a hike or something."

"No. I'll lose them on my own. I don't want to make a play for them until I can figure out a few more things."

"Okay." Bo tapped the piece of paper with the Mazda's license number. "You want me to go any deeper on this, or just the name?"

"Just the name, Bo. It's not a paying gig."

"That's what the Indian said. It's supposed to make a difference? Look, just because Sweet burned you, it doesn't mean that all your friends are fuck-ups."

"Yeah. I know that. Sorry, Bo."

"Next time, *you* call me — don't wait for Jimmy to do it for you."

Swann nodded. He went to the front window of the apartment and looked down on Bank Street. The Buick was parked across the street in front of the IGA. He checked the time. Going on to nine-thirty. He had time to lose them before he connected with this Skiv character.

"I'll see you later," he said.

Bo nodded. "Keep it hanging, Jake. And give a thought to your little fiddler. You never know. It could be the start of a beautiful thing."

"What are you? Ann Landers all of a sudden?"

"Fuck you, Jake."

"Now that's the Bo Jeffries I've come to know and love." Swann headed for the door. "When you get a name to go with that number, just leave it with Sue, okay?"

"'Know and love?'" Bo asked. "Is that like in the Biblical sense? Because I don't know, Jake. You're not really my type, you know what I mean? Though maybe if you'd wear that blonde wig of yours more often..."

Swann closed the door on him and took the stairs down.

Thirteen

The Buick that had followed Swann from the hospital was still parked across the street when he stepped onto the sidewalk. He started across the pavement towards it. Before he reached the center line, the car pulled away, passed Fourth Avenue, and turned left on Fifth. Swann knew they'd be turning, hoping to pick him up in his car when he drove off. Still looking south on Bank, Swann smiled and returned to the side of the street that his apartment was on. A bus was coming. He kept his eye on the corner of Fifth and Bank, dropped his $1.10 in the fare box when the bus stopped for him and hurried to a seat on his right. He slouched low and peered back. As the bus was pulling away, he could see the Buick nosing around the corner of Fifth. It was still there when the bus took him out of sight.

Swann straightened up in his seat and rode the bus north to Cooper Street. He got off there and started to check the house numbers, but gave up when he heard the sound of the party.

The house was lit up, both floors. What passed for music didn't so much spill from its open doors and windows as knife out. Swann frowned as he went up the steps onto the porch. Christ, he really was getting too old.

There was a girl in her teens drinking a beer beside the front door. She lounged against the house, her heavy makeup looking like a mask in the light from the street lamps. She had bare feet, black leather pants, and a T-shirt with the arms torn off. Her hair was a kaleidoscope of orange, black and peroxide blonde. A set of handcuffs held together the two ends of a belt that hung low around her skinny hips. Beyond her were two males, neither of them much older than she. One wore army fatigues and a vest, the other worn jeans, torn at the knees. He was barechested.

"I'm looking for a guy named Skiv," he told the girl.

"So?"

"Is he here?"

She jerked her head towards the door.

"Any chance you could get him for me?"

"What do I look like?" she asked. "A fucking butler?"

More like something the cat dragged in, Swann thought.

"I'll get him," one of the boys said.

Swann looked over to them. It was the one in the army fatigues who'd spoken up. "Thanks."

"You got a name he'd know?"

"Swann."

The girl giggled. The boy in the army fatigues grinned with her, but he brushed by Swann and went inside. He came back a minute or so later with Skiv in tow.

Swann's first impression of Skiv was that he looked like a rooster — one that might have a lot of jailtime in his future. The orange Mohawk looked like a multipointed cock's comb. His skin was so pale he looked dead. His nose was like a beak, sharp and pointed, his eyes small and nervous. He dressed in jeans and black boots and a T-shirt that said, "If it ain't Stiff, it ain't worth a fuck." Swann recognized it as the logo of an independent record company based in England. The record store where he bought his Celtic records used to sell those shirts.

"You the guy looking for Knickers?" Skiv asked.

"Knickers?"

"The girl in the picture Cohen had."

Swann nodded. "Why do you call her that?"

"Because she never wore any."

The comment elicited another giggle from the girl by the door.

"And Skiv's short for skivvies?" Swann asked. "Because you do wear them?"

"I don't have to talk to you," Skiv said.

He started to go back inside, but Swann caught his arm and pulled him back. "Let's walk," he said.

Skiv hesitated a moment, then nodded. "Sure. Why not?"

He led the way down the steps.

"So you're a detective?" he asked as they reached the sidewalk. "What do you call yourselves? Private dicks?"

"You know any public ones?"

"Just what I see on TV."

Skiv gave Swann a once-over. Swann was dressed in jeans, a light blue cotton shirt and a summer-weight sport jacket. Everything he wore, down to his scuffed shoes, was frayed and worn.

"Not much money in your line of work?" Skiv asked.

"What do you know about the girl?" Swann said.

"What's to know? She blew into town maybe three, four weeks ago—up from T.O. She was young and she was stupid, but she could fuck like a bunny."

Old man Menzies was going to love this, Swann thought.

"You know where I can find her?" he asked.

Skiv shook his head. "Haven't seen her for a week or so. Say, what's all this shit worth to you anyway? Cohen said you were paying."

"So far you've earned yourself about ten cents."

"Hey, I'm doing my best, man."

Swann thought for a few moments. "She still look the same—like in the picture where she's got the Mohawk?"

"She'd shaved her head, last time I saw her—looked good once the stubble started. I think she was maybe turning tricks—that help?"

"Where? On the Market?"

"No. The strip on Bank around Barrymore's."

"Did she have a pimp?"

"I don't know for sure that she was even taking money, you know? I just saw her with a couple of straight guys a couple of times — once getting into a car, once getting out."

"What did they look like?"

"Older guys — your age."

Thanks a lot, Swann thought.

"Any idea where I could start looking for her?"

"Try the Rideau Centre. All the young nouveau-punks are hanging out there these days. You know them — they live in suburbia, but they've got all the gear. Leather and chains. Making a statement."

"You don't sound as though you think too much of them."

"Hey, what's to think?" Skiv asked. "This is 1985, man. Things've changed. Most everybody's fucked off to Vancouver. All we got left is the chickenshits. Part-time punks. They don't want to give up mommie and daddy's nice big house and bread, but they want to get down and be a little weird at the same time."

"Like weekend hippies."

Skiv nodded. "That's your era? Maybe you're not so old, then. You just look so fucking straight."

He grabbed Swann's arm and gave it a squeeze.

"You might as well be a cop," he added. "What do you do, eat muscle sandwiches?"

"I work out some."

Skiv shook his head. "Bet it's just loads of fun."

"So most of the punks are just phonies — is that what you're saying?" Swann asked, trying to steer the conversation back to something he could use.

"What am I up to now?" Skiv asked. "Ten bucks yet?"

"Five-fifty."

"Shit, man. What do you *want*?"

"Something I can use."

"Okay. We used to have some clubs, houses—that kinda shit—but it's all faded. Sid's dead and he ain't coming back. There's just no real hardcore left. I mean you still get a few sounds outta England, like the Exploited, say, but most of what we get in this city now comes up from the States. The Dead Kennedys are still going strong. There's the Black Flag. The Minute Men. But it's just not the same."

"What are you saying?"

"That you're looking in the wrong place for Knickers. She was hardcore—just a stupid kid, but she didn't do things halfway. So I'm guessing she blew. Vancouver, maybe. Maybe the States."

"Why'd you never go? What keeps you here?"

"I'll tell you. Here, I'm somebody. I'm important. All the neo-punks know me and look up to me. I go someplace else and I'm just another asshole—you understand? What I've got here is a little prestige."

Swann glanced at him sharply, startled at the moment of honesty. "You're pretty sure she left town then?" he asked.

"If she's still here, she's invisible."

"Okay. Thanks." Swann handed him a ten.

"This is *it?*"

"You didn't exactly tell me a whole lot I couldn't have worked out for myself."

They were stopped at the corner of Cooper and Bronson. Skiv looked down at the ten.

"You ever hear of Marc Bedard?" he asked.

Swann shook his head.

"He makes films—hardcore, but we're talking a different kinda hardcore now, understand?"

"Porn?"

"You got it. Now a lotta straight guys like to see a film where one of them's banging the shit outta some little punkette. Maybe they just go for all the chains and leather—I don't know."

"Trish worked for him?"

"Trish? What kinda fucking name is that? Girl I knew named Knickers did a little work for him. Her parents hire you?"

Swann shrugged.

"You tell them the kid they knew's dead. Somebody they don't know — somebody they're never gonna know — is walking around in her body."

"If I see them I'll tell them that."

"Give it to 'em straight, man. Anarchy's all that makes sense now. Shake 'em up a little. Do 'em some good."

"This Bedard — does he have an office?"

"Are you kidding? You expecting some little sign that says 'Porn films made here?' Get serious."

"So where do I find him?"

"What am I up to now?"

"We're working on thirty bucks."

"Let's work on forty."

Swann studied him. Skiv stood with his hands in his pockets and met Swann's gaze with a sullen look in his small eyes.

"Okay," Swann said. "We're working on forty now."

"You know the Eastway Gardens — off Tremblay Road?"

Swann nodded.

"He's got a place on Avenue 'R.'" Skiv gave Swann the house number. "That's where he makes his flicks. It's a real private sort of a deal. He gets orders and makes up a special film — all on video. Name your perversion, understand? He probably keeps dupes for himself, but they're pretty well one-of-a-kind items."

"How rough is this stuff?"

Skiv shook his head. "Not necessarily rough. It's just that the guys who go for this kinda shit like to think they've got the only copy. Like I said, Bedard's probably got dupes — he's semi-twisted himself — but he doesn't sell the same flick twice."

"How do you know all this?"

Skiv grinned. "Hey. I'm something of a film star myself."

Swann pulled out a couple of twenties and handed them over.

"Okay," he said. "Thanks for your time."

Skiv crumpled the twenties and stuck them in his pocket. "Anytime, Mr. Dick."

Swann started to walk away, but Skiv caught his arm. When Swann turned, the punk let his hand drop. It went back into his pocket.

"One thing," he said. "Word gets back to Bedard on where you heard this and —" the hand came out of his pocket with a switchblade that opened with a click. "You're not going to look so pretty."

Swann studied him for a moment, then smiled. Before Skiv could do anything, Swann hit the knife hand with the side of his own left. The knife dropped out of nerveless fingers and hit the pavement with a clatter.

"Hey —" Skiv began.

Swann gathered up Skiv's T-shirt and lifted the punk onto his toes.

"Don't ever pull a knife on me again," he said softly.

"S-sure..."

Swann let him go with a push and Skiv backpedalled to keep his balance. Turning, Swann kicked the knife out into the middle of the street and walked away.

"Fuck you, too!" Skiv shouted after him.

Swann never bothered to turn around.

Fourteen

The dark brown Buick was parked in front of the IGA once more when Swann disembarked from the southbound bus. He gave a jaunty salute to the two men in the car. Neither of them acknowledged it. They weren't the same two men that had attacked him last night — they couldn't be the same; not unless he'd lost his touch — but they were cut from a similar cloth.

When he got upstairs he found Bo still there.

"There's beer in the fridge. Help yourself."

Swann shook his head in weary resignation. "Making yourself at home?"

"Figured I'd sleep on your couch tonight. You had visitors while you were gone."

"Oh?" Swann got himself a Bud, Sooey at his heels, and brought it back into the living room.

"They hit the buzzer and didn't seem too happy when I was here to answer it."

Swann nodded. It was one of the many things he'd learned from Bo. Before you broke into a place, you either phoned ahead or rang the bell. It sure beat finding somebody home when you didn't want anybody to be there. Swann only used the information he got from Bo to help him in his line of work. Bo, after doing time and seeing he could do okay working with Swann, had pretty much mended his ways now as well.

"So what did they have to say?" Swann asked.

"Had the wrong place," Bo replied with a grin. "I gave 'em a good look at Sooey who managed a pretty convincing growl, then went to the window and watched them climb back into their car."

"Any idea what they were looking for?"

Bo shook his head. "I left Sooey on guard and got us some more brew across the river. I doubt they tried the place again while I was gone."

They wouldn't, Swann thought. Not without leaving a piece of themselves behind. Sooey could do more than look convincing.

"What about you?" Bo asked.

Swann filled him in.

"I got a feeling about this," Bo said, "and it's not good."

"You know Bedard?"

"I've heard of him. He's got some official connections. Guys he provides a service for — a lot of them are big wheels. Federal, some of them. Definitely some municipal. He's also got some connections that aren't so official."

"I just want the girl."

Bo nodded. "Yeah. But a guy like that — wouldn't you like to take him down?"

"Be a pleasure," Swann said.

"So what's next?"

"Check Bedard out, I guess."

"You gonna talk to him?"

Swann shook his head. "Thought I might like to have a look at his place first."

"I'd like to get in on that. You going tonight?"

"Tomorrow night." Swann took a swig of his beer and finally gave in and let Sooey up on the chair with him. He grunted as the terrier set its weight on his lap. He scratched the dog behind the ears. "What do you want in for?"

Bo shrugged. "People who are old enough to know better —
I figure it's their problem whatever they get into. But kids...I
don't like a guy like that, Jake."

"You're hoping he's going to be home."

"Naw. I just want to get some shit on him and then run
him out of town."

"If he's got connections..."

"First he's got to connect with 'em, Jake. I'd like to work
this as a side deal — just for personal satisfaction. Isn't that
what you're always going on to me about? To get some
satisfaction out of my job?"

Swann smiled. "Let's just get the kid out first."

"Sure. That's no problem. What about Rankin?"

"I'm still thinking about him."

"Guy's a cop," Bo said. "That's gonna make it hard to take
him down."

"I know. But he's not getting away with what he did to
Sammy."

"I didn't say he should. We just have to handle this right,
or we'll be up to our asses in heat. Cops stick close together."

Swann thought about Lou Sweet sitting at Rankin's kitchen
table, sharing a brew. He frowned and pushed Sooey from his
lap. Finishing his beer, he stood up.

"Yeah," he said. "They do that."

"What're we gonna do about your shadows outside?" Bo
asked.

Swann glanced through the window to see the Buick still
parked in front of the IGA.

"I'm going to bed," he said.

The next morning it was raining and the Buick was gone. Swann managed a passable thanks to Sue for his wake-up call, shaved and had a shower. Afterwards he called the hospital and then told Bo he was going downstairs for breakfast.

"How's your girlfriend?" Bo asked.

"I'm springing her today."

"Good. I'll leave word with Sue if I get anything on the Mazda's plates."

Swann grunted acknowledgement. He had a brief tussle at the door with Sooey who wanted to follow him downstairs, but he finally managed to get out and make it down to his table at The Avenue Restaurant on his own. Forty-five minutes later he was at the General Hospital, walking beside the wheelchair that an orderly pushed to the front door. Jimmy Crackle brought the car around and Swann helped Sammy into the front seat. The rain had let up, but the sky remained overcast. The air was filled with a clean, wet smell.

"I've been thinking," Swann said, once Jimmy was in the back seat and he'd started up the Acadian. "You don't want to be alone, right?"

Sammy shook her head.

"Well, I've got a couple of things to run down today, but I know someone you can stay with if you want to."

"Who's that?"

"A lady by the name of Sue Wheeler."

Sammy blinked. "Answering service Sue?"

"That's her. What do you think?"

"I suppose…"

"I guarantee you'll be safe at her place and I'll be by early in the afternoon. We can see how things are going then."

"Can I get a few things at home?"

"You betcha."

He took Smyth until it crossed the Rideau River and turned into Main Street. Main took them to Colonel by Drive. They let Jimmy out where it met Rideau Street and became Sussex Drive. The fairly new and still impressive Rideau Centre, a multilevel shopping concourse that seemed largely composed of shoe stores whenever Swann was in it, loomed over them as Jimmy disembarked from the Acadian.

"I'll see you tonight," Jimmy said.

"I'm not sure where I'll be," Swann said. He didn't really want to get Jimmy involved in the illegal activities that he and Bo had planned for the night.

"Don't worry," Jimmy Crackle said. "I'll find you."

And he would, Swann thought as he drove off down Sussex towards Sammy's apartment on Clarence behind the old fish store. Swann parked in the lane.

"What do you have to do today?" Sammy asked.

"It's just a missing persons case that I took on before I'd heard what happened to you. Sixteen-year-old kid from Toronto. Listen, Sammy. I'm sorry but—"

"That's okay, Jake. God, you've done more than your share already."

"I told you—that's what friends are for."

Sammy smiled. "You've been a good one. And so has Jimmy. He was telling me about the reserve he grew up on and hunting up north…Between the two of you, I've hardly had time to think about…you know…"

"That's good, Sammy," he said, returning her smile. "Hey, you'll have to tell me some of the stuff Jimmy told you. He's so close-mouthed with me you'd think I was auditing him for Revenue Canada."

"Sure. But you know, I don't know what I'd have…what I'd do…"

Tears welled in her eyes and Swann didn't try to jolly her anymore. There was a time for that kind of thing, but this wasn't it. He put an arm awkwardly around her shoulders. There really wasn't much to her, he thought. She was always thin, but the past couple of days had really taken their toll.

"C'mon, Sammy," he said. "You've got to be strong now. Those guys took a piece of you, but if you're not strong, they'll get to keep it. That's what those kinds of guys want. They want you to just keep thinking about it, they want you to always be afraid of it happening again, but you can't let the bastards win. You're still you. You pulled through. You've got to go with that now. Take it a day at a time."

"That…that's what Jimmy said too."

Swann nodded. "I know what you're going through. The kind of work I do puts me in contact with a lot of hurting people. The ones that make it are the ones that learn to carry on. Like Sue Wheeler. Wait'll you meet her. The accident took away the use of her legs, the other driver's insurance company screwed her and then went bankrupt…She's an inspiration, Sammy. No question."

"I guess…when you put it like that."

Swann held her a little closer. "Hey," he said softly. "I'm not saying you don't have as much cause to hurt as she did, Sammy. I'm just saying that you've got to put it behind you now. You've got to at least give it a try. And we're all going to help you."

For a long moment she rested her head against his shoulder. The odd sniffle punctuated her breathing.

"Thanks," she said finally, her voice husky. "Jeez, Jake…"

"C'mon," he said. "Let's get your stuff."

They packed a small bag. Sammy was going to leave her fiddle behind, but Swann shook his head and tucked it under his arm. She didn't protest.

Outside, Swann had a good long look for the Buick. On the way to Sue's, he constantly checked the rearview mirror for it, or anybody else tailing them. If they were there, they were good. He couldn't spot them.

Twenty minutes later they were pulling up in front of Sue Wheeler's ground floor apartment on Elgin Street near Waverly.

Any misgivings or shyness that Sammy had felt about coming to stay with a complete stranger, vanished as soon as Sue opened the door. Sue wheeled her chair backwards, face filled with concern, but going easy on the sympathy. She knew from her own experience how too much of that was harder to take than none at all.

"Come on in," she said. "The place is a mess but then—"

"It always is," Swann finished for her.

Sue laughed. The two women regarded each other while Swann made the introductions. Sue's apartment was small, without a great deal in the way of furniture. What there was, was widely spaced so that she could easily maneuver her wheelchair around the obstructions. A woman who lived upstairs helped her with her meals and shopping, but otherwise Sue operated entirely on her own.

"I'll show you where you can put your things," Sue said and rolled her wheelchair down a short hall to the bedroom. "We'll have to share, I'm afraid, and you'll be sleeping on the couch—I hope you like a hard bed."

"I love it," Sammy said. She slept on a mattress on the floor at her own apartment which was furnished circa Haight-Ashbury, the Summer of Love.

Swann waited until they came back into the living room before leaving. "I should be back around two," he said.

"Don't forget to give my message to Wes," Sammy said.

Swann nodded. "Two-thirty, then. You're going to be okay —
both of you?"

The two women exchanged glances.

"We're going to be fine," Sue said.

Sammy nodded. "Thanks again, Jake."

"Hey. I expect a lot of free dinners out of this," he said with
a smile.

When he closed the door, Sammy was sitting on the couch,
Sue in her wheelchair near her, and they were already talking
comfortably. More than staying with him, Swann thought, this
was what Sammy really needed. Another woman to talk to.

When he hit the street, he checked for the Buick, but it still
hadn't picked him up again yet. He got into the Acadian and
pulled away from the curb. It wasn't until he was delivering
Sammy's message to her friend Wes, that he found out that
Happy Cohen was dead.

Wes Thompson was of that indeterminate age somewhere between nineteen and twenty-seven. He had dirty-blonde hair cut short above his collar and a pair of round wire-framed glasses. His features were softened by a slight chubbiness. He wore a collarless cotton shirt and drawstring pants. Swann found him in the short pedestrian's underpass on the south side of Rideau that led from Confederation Square to Rideau Street. He was playing the guitar and just finishing up a version of Stan Rogers' "White Squall."

A good strong voice, Swann thought, but he guessed that wasn't enough. There was less than five dollars in change in the open guitar case. Either Thompson wasn't to the taste of the passersby, or they were just getting too jaded. Every summer there were more and more buskers — musicians, acrobats, jugglers, magicians and you name it — vying for their loose change.

Swann dropped a couple of quarters in the guitar case and delivered his message.

"How's she doing anyway?" Wes asked.

"She's going to be okay."

"It's a goddamn shame, you know? Sammy's such a good kid."

"Yeah. But it happens all the same."

Wes shook his head. "I don't know who I'm going to get to replace her for that gig. She's the reason we got it in the first place. It's not like there was a hell of a lot of money up for grabs, but a gig's a gig."

"There's got to be other fiddlers around town," Swann said.

"Yeah. But none with her class. She puts a lift into everything she plays."

Swann shrugged. There wasn't a whole lot more he could say. He looked out at the passersby and suddenly caught sight of Jimmy Crackle.

"I'll see you around," he told Wes.

"Give Sammy my best—okay?"

Swann nodded. He was already on his way to where Jimmy was waiting for him. Jimmy had a serious look on his face.

"What's up?" Swann asked.

"It's Happy Cohen, Jevon. He was killed early this morning."

"Killed?"

"Hit and run."

"Shit. Anybody see it happen?"

"Don't know," Jimmy Crackle replied. "The police are supposed to have taken a statement from somebody."

Swann sighed. "So the only way we're going to find out fast..."

"You'll have to call Sweet," Jimmy said. He shook his head at the tension in Swann's face at the mention of Lou Sweet's name. "Just put on a white man's smile and give him a call. It won't be hard."

A white man's smile was Jimmy Crackle's catch-all for smiling when you were about to lie to someone or cheat them.

"No," Swann said. "Not hard at all."

They headed west on Rideau until they found a phone booth and Swann put the call through. Lou Sweet was in his office.

"Swann," Lou said cheerfully. "How's your friend?"

"She's doing fine."

"And your case?"

"It's going fine, too." Christ, it was hard to stay civil. "I'm calling about Happy Cohen, Lou. I just heard. What's the word?"

"What's Happy Cohen got to do with you?"

"He was a friend."

"You've got some weird friends, Swann."

"Fercrissakes, Lou. The man's dead."

"You're right. Shouldn't speak ill of them and all that shit. It was a hit and run, Swann."

"You got anything on the car?"

"Not much. We've got one witness — a wino. Goes by the name of Legs Larry — you know him?"

"Yeah."

"He said it was a dark-coloured Buick did the job. Just came right up on the curb and picked Cohen off, then tore away."

"Did he get a plate number?"

"What do *you* think?"

Swann was thinking about a dark brown Buick that had been parked across from his apartment for most of the night.

"Any idea about what time it happened?" he asked.

"Around five A.M. You've got an awful lot of interest about a guy who was just a fucking informer, Swann."

"You figure that's what happened? He got hit?"

"Everybody knew what kind of business he was in. My guess is he sold one secret too many."

Swann tried to read Lou Sweet's voice. Was there a warning in it?

"Yeah, well, thanks, Lou. I'll be in touch."

"Swann, are you mixed up in this?"

"What do you mean?"

"Don't play coy with me, pal. If you've got something on this, I want it."

"First I heard of it was ten minutes ago, Lou."

"Well, if you do hear anything, you let me know."

"I'll do that. See you around."

Swann hung up before the conversation could drift back into something personal. He just didn't think he could keep that "white man's smile" going much longer.

"It was the Buick," he told Jimmy as he stepped away from the booth.

Jimmy Crackle had just finished rolling a cigarette. He stuck it between his lips and flicked a wooden match with his thumbnail, dragging on the homemade cigarette.

"That's all?" he asked.

"Legs Larry saw it go down."

"He was probably drunk."

Swann nodded. "But he knows his cars. He used to be a mechanic."

"Are you going to talk to him?"

"No. I don't think I'd get anything more out of him."

"Probably not." Jimmy Crackle lifted a hand to Swann. "I'll see you later, Jevon."

"Sure. Happy trails."

He watched Jimmy leave, then turned to the Rideau Street doors of the shopping centre. He spent the next hour or so trying to match the faces of the young punks hanging out in the mall to the two photos he was still carrying in the pocket of his sport jacket. He didn't have much luck. He kept thinking about Cohen and feeling bad.

There could have been any number of people who were unhappy enough with Cohen to call a hit on him, but Swann was pretty sure it was connected with him. Either Cohen had gotten too close to something, or the hit was a warning. But a warning about what? To lay off the search for Trish Menzies, or something more subtle? Like don't get too close to Bob Rankin? A guy that'd do what he'd done to Sammy…Swann wouldn't put much past him. Or his friends. Like Lou Sweet.

He tried showing the photos to some of the punks with predictable results. The first one he tried was a young girl who couldn't have been more than fourteen. She had jet-black hair, spiked on one side of her head, the other half of her head shaved bald. A quarter inch of stubble had already grown back in. Her makeup was black over her eyes, dark red rouge lined like warpaint on her cheeks. She was wearing a ratty old Vice Squad T-shirt and a black leather miniskirt.

"Do you know this girl?" he asked her, showing her the pictures.

"Who wants to know?"

Swann was getting tired of their tough poses.

"I do, asshole. Do you know her?"

"Fuck off, cop."

After awhile he did, checking in with one of the mall's security guards before he left. He showed the man his ID. The guard was young, clean-shaven and short-haired, but slouching in his uniform. The slouch threw off the neat impression that the uniform should have made.

"Yeah," he said. "I've seen her around. But not lately. You working for her parents?"

Swann nodded. He could see that the guard was torn between the generation that his uniform represented and the one that Trish Menzies belonged to. It couldn't have been that long since he was on the younger side of the fence.

"Not a bad looking kid," the guard added. "Clean her up a little and give her a couple of years..."

Swann thought of middle-aged men paying Marc Bedard to deliver their fantasies to them. Fantasies that included kids like Trish.

"Thanks anyway," he said.

He decided it was time to get back to Sue's. Maybe Bo had already phoned in with some information on the Mazda's plates.

He left the Rideau Centre, intending to go collect his car parked behind the old police station. As he stepped out of the Nicholas Street entrance, a boy in his mid-teens stopped him. He had the punk uniform down to a T. The Mohawk, a big silver bomb-shaped earring hanging from his right earlobe, a sleeveless plain black T-shirt and jeans, torn at the knee. He looked too young to be shaving yet, but his grey eyes had a look in them that told Swann that he'd been around some.

"You're the guy that's looking for Knickers, right?"

Swann nodded.

"And you were at Cooper Street last night—talking to Skiv?"

"Right again. What's your name?"

"Johnny."

"Johnny what?"

"Just Johnny—it doesn't matter. Did Skiv tell you about Bedard—the guy that makes the movies?"

"He told me. He said she'd done a couple for him. That he'd done some, too."

"Yeah, well, it's a way to make a buck. Beats selling your ass on the street."

"You do that?"

"Movies or selling my ass?"

"They're pretty much the same thing, wouldn't you say?"

"And you're a pretty smart fucking guy, aren't you?" Johnny said. "You want to hear what I got to say, or not?"

"I'm listening."

"Knickers used to be around a lot—she's from Toronto, you know? Last time I saw her she was getting into a car with Bedard and a couple of other guys and I haven't seen her since."

"When was this?"

"Last week. No—two weeks ago, now. A Wednesday night."

"Where was it?"

Johnny pointed down towards the Market. "On York Street. We were heading out to a party when the car pulled over and Bedard asked her if she wanted to make a few bucks. She got in and they were gone."

"Thanks," Swann said. He reached into his pocket and came up with a twenty that he tried to hand over.

"Hey, fuck your money, man."

"If you don't want the money, then why are you telling me all this?"

"I like Knickers and I think she's in trouble, that's all. A guy like me, I can't do a whole fuck of a lot for her — not up against Bedard and the guys he runs around with. But I've heard about you. I figure if I could point you in the right direction, maybe you'd be able to help her."

"And bring her back to you?"

"Hey, fuck, man — what's with you? I'm trying to help somebody. Not you, but Knickers. Okay?"

Swann stuck the twenty back in his pocket. "Okay," he said. "Thanks for your help." He started to go, then paused. "What if your help just sends her back to her parents?"

Johnny shrugged. "Beats being dead. Besides, she can always take off from them again if she doesn't like it."

"You think she's dead?" Swann asked.

"I don't know, man. All I know is she's not around. Maybe she blew town. Sometimes Bedard has some pretty important guys that want to be in the flicks themselves with whatever's going down. Times like that, you don't see the girls anymore. Now I'm not saying he's killing 'em off, but shit, man. Where do they go?"

"I don't know," Swann said. He was starting to get a sick feeling in the pit of his stomach. "But I'm going to find out."

"You do that. And give the fucker one for Johnny when you do."

Swann nodded. He left Johnny standing there by the entrance to the Rideau Centre and went for his car. Maybe the punks weren't all bad, he thought as he coaxed the Acadian to start. It took a minute or so before the engine turned over and then coughed into life. Or maybe the punks had something against Bedard and were setting Swann up against him because they figured they couldn't do anything to him themselves. One way or another, though, Swann meant to find out what had happened to Trish Menzies. But also what was going down with Mark Bedard and his little film industry.

The picture of Bedard that was forming in Swann's mind was getting uglier by the minute. He wasn't so sure he wanted to find out what had happened to the Menzies girl now—he was afraid of what he was going to find. But he wasn't going to stop looking for her.

Seventeen

There was a message from Bo for Swann when he arrived at Sue's apartment. He spent a few minutes chatting with the two women, then made the call. The number Bo had left was Swann's own.

"Are you moving in or something?" he asked when Bo came on the line.

"I just cleaned my own place yesterday, Jake. I thought I'd go for a record and have it clean for a few days in a row."

"Thanks a lot. So I've got to suffer?"

"Keep it up, Jake, and I'll have Sooey dump one on your rug."

"I always wondered if that dog'd taste like pork. So what've you got for me?"

"My friend ran down the plate number. It's registered to the Bourget Corporation."

"I've never heard of it."

"Welcome to the club. I checked it out and it's some kind of investment company. The office is on Wellington — down in the West End."

"So we don't have a name to go with the guy I saw at Rankin's."

"Not yet. I could find out."

"You're not busy?"

"Not so busy I can't check this out, Jake. Are we still on for tonight?"

"Yeah. Bedard's starting to look less and less pretty as the day goes by. You hear about Cohen?"

"Yeah. Do you think it's connected?"

"I don't know," Swann said. "It feels like it."

"A lotta guys could've had a hard-on for Cohen."

"That's what Lou said."

There was a moment's silence. "You were talking to him?" Bo asked.

"Yeah."

"And?"

"And nothing. I'll see you tonight, Bo. My place."

"I can hardly wait. You hear that, Sooey? I've got a date."

Swann hung up, a smile twitching at the corner of his mouth.

He spent an hour or so with Sammy and Sue, then told them he had to go and get ready for some business he had to take care of that night. Sammy walked him to the door. She wasn't moving so stiffly anymore.

"How are you doing?" Swann asked.

"Better—especially since I got out of that hospital. I felt like I was in prison."

Swann smiled. "Yeah. It gives you that feeling, doesn't it? How's your tooth?"

"I'm getting it capped next week. Right now I'm living on painkillers."

"Lovely. What do you have on for the afternoon?"

"We're going to play some music. Did you know that Sue plays classical guitar? She practices six hours *every* day."

"No shit?"

He glanced down the hall to where he could see Sue putting their coffee mugs on the kitchen counter.

"She likes you, you know."

"Yeah, well, we're friends."

"But I like you better," Sammy said.

Swann just looked at her. He didn't know what to say. He wasn't sure if Sammy was just hanging on to him because he was something solid in a world that had suddenly gone ugly on her, or if she'd always felt that way and the attack had loosened something inside her that had kept her from telling him before. He wasn't sure how he felt about it either.

"Everybody likes me," he said lightly. "I'm just that kind of guy."

Sammy leaned against him for a moment.

"We're going to have to talk about all of this one of these days," she said.

She went up on her toes and kissed Swann on the lips, a quick hard kiss, and then she was backing away from him. He could see something warring in her eyes. The care she felt for him. The fear of men that Rankin's brutal attack had left in her. There were a lot of things that were going to need working out — for both of them.

"You take care, Sammy," he said.

The warmth of her smile and the memory of her lips on his stayed with him all the way on the drive home.

Eighteen

Sooey bounded across the living room of Swann's apartment and lunged for him, trying to climb up Swann's leg as he came in the front door.

"Did you ever think of walking him?" Swann asked.

"Thought I'd give you the pleasure. I've got some background on the Bourget Corp."

Swann shook his head. "Let me get a beer."

He disappeared into the kitchen and came back with a Budweiser for each of them.

"So shoot," he said as he settled in the chair by the window.

He pushed Sooey away from his lap and ignored the pained expression on the dog's face as it slumped on the floor and watched him.

"Danny Poirier's the main shareholder."

"Shit."

"I know what you mean," Bo said.

Daniel Poirier had started out as a small-time hood with his fingers in the drug trade. For awhile he'd dabbled in prostitution—running a string of high class hookers—and pornography. Since the advent of the popularity of home video machines, he'd been making moves into the lucrative business of hardcore porn cassettes. The trouble with Poirier was that he had connections with organized crime in Toronto and

Montreal. Word on the street had it that he was just a front for the mob.

"Cohen would have known," Swann said.

"Yeah."

"Thing is, that car was parked at Rankin's."

Bo nodded. "But knowing Poirier, I'll bet he's tied into the business with Bedard as well."

"I don't like it."

"You don't have to like it, Jake. It's just the way things are working out."

The truth of that didn't make it easier for Swann to take.

"Where'd you get this?" he asked.

"I plugged into Peter Benford down at *The Citizen*. He dropped off some photocopies of what they had in their Morgue."

"Let's see what you've got."

Bo handed over the manila envelope that Benford had left him. The first sheet Swann pulled out was a picture of the man he'd seen at Rankin's. A caption underneath identified him as Keith Weppler. He was another shareholder in the Bourget Corporation. Also its accountant.

Swann scanned the rest of the information contained on the photocopied pages in the envelope. According to what they had on file at *The Citizen,* the corporation dealt with real estate, stocks and bonds, owned two restaurants, a strip club, a recording studio, two exercise clubs, and a movie production company. The latter was called Sigouin-Bedard Productions. They specialized in TV ads and other commercial work. Right.

Swann looked up. "Did you read all of this?"

Bo nodded.

Swann went back to finish it himself. Marcel Sigouin was also a shareholder of the Bourget Corporation. Bedard wasn't. The two other shareholders were Victorin Lavallee and Glen Foster. The first owned a couple of clubs over on the Hull side. The latter had a construction company. Nowhere in the information was there any talk of mob connections. But Swann knew enough to read between the lines. Where it said "alleged" and "suspected," you read that they just hadn't been caught with their pants down yet. And it helped to have cops like Rankin and Lou Sweet in your pocket.

"Benford ask you why you wanted this stuff?" he asked as he laid it aside.

"Sure. But he owes me. He knows if we come up with something he can use, we'll give him first crack."

Swann sighed. He finished his beer and went into the kitchen for another. When he came back, he stood at the window for a few moments. The Buick was still gone. It wouldn't be back. Not with a smashed-in fender that could connect it to Happy Cohen's murder—just saying the police even bothered to follow up on it. If Sweet was in charge of the case, it would probably get filed away, end of story.

"That blue Lincoln was sitting out there for a couple of hours earlier," Bo said.

Swann checked his watch. He hadn't noticed it on his way in, but he saw that it was past five-thirty now. From three-thirty to five-thirty in the afternoon, that was a tow-away zone.

"More babysitters?" he asked.

"Same pair—new car. I went across the street to get us a couple of steaks for supper and checked them out."

"We'll have to lose them if we're going to hit Bedard's tonight."

"That's still on?"

Swann nodded. "Christ, this is getting messy. All I want is Rankin and whoever was with him that night. Rankin—and the Menzies girl delivered back to her old man. This is getting too deep for us. I don't know how tight Poirier's connections are, but the mob can field a hell of a lot more men than we can."

"Hell," Bo said. "Let 'em come. We've got Sooey on our side."

Swann turned to look at Sooey. The dog had lifted its head at the sound of its name.

"Right," he said.

"We've gotta do it," Bo said. "If we back down now, we're not gonna look good, and if we don't look good, we don't get any business."

"It's the personal stake I've got in it that's bothering me. That and the way that what happened to Sammy is suddenly all tied up with my looking for the Menzies kid."

"You know what the Indian says—everything's a part of the same pattern. We just don't see the connections most of the time."

Swann nodded. "That's the way it usually works out, all right."

"So we're on?"

"For tonight at least. After we hit Bedard's place, we'll have to stop and take a good look at just what the hell it is that we're getting into."

Swann turned back to the window and stared down at the Lincoln and its passengers. Bo studied his back for a few moments, then stood up.

"I'll fix those steaks," he said.

Swann nodded, but he didn't turn around.

B o went out the back door and down the fire escape, Sooey at his heels. He found Jimmy Crackle waiting for him at the bottom. Swann watched them both get into Bo's battered old Ford Econoline van and drive off. He gave them five minutes, then went downstairs to where he'd parked his Acadian on Bank Street. He didn't pay any attention to the Lincoln still parked in front of the IGA, but he heard its engine start up as he got into his own car.

The Acadian started immediately for a change and Swann wondered if that was an omen. If so, was it a good one or a bad one? He decided that he didn't much care at this point.

He pushed in a cassette and the jaunty fiddling of Johnny Doherty filled the car. The cassette had been made from a 1978 Gael Linn recording, though the actual music had been recorded three years previously. Doherty had literally been born a fiddler — if the story he told about his birth was true. The midwife had laid him down on the top of a dresser moments after he was born and what did he do but pick up his father's bow, holding it between his thumb and forefinger.

Swann smiled. He liked that story. He liked the tune that was playing now, too.

It was a Scottish strathspey called "The Cat That Kittled in Jamie's Wig." He wasn't all that sure what the title meant. Sammy had told him that it referred to a cat that had her kittens in somebody's wig, but Swann had his own idea. His smile grew a little broader. Christ knew he needed a few laughs these days.

He pulled a U-turn and headed south on Bank Street. Checking the rearview, he saw the Lincoln give him a block lead, then fall dutifully in behind him. Swann tapped his steering wheel in time to the strathspey. He picked up a little speed as he passed Lansdowne Park, making the Lincoln work a little to keep up with him. He crossed the bridge over the Rideau Canal. Because of the slight rise, he was out of the Lincoln's view for a couple of minutes on the far side of the bridge. He floored the gas pedal. The Acadian reacted sluggishly, but by the time the Lincoln topped the rise, Swann had another block's lead on them.

He caught the light at Sunnyside on the amber, but doubted that a red light would stop his tail. Belmont Avenue was coming up. Just before the Bank of Nova Scotia, Swann stepped hard on the brakes and turned left into the bank's parking lot. He went to the end of it and turned right down a short alley that led onto Belmont. When he reached the end of the alley, he killed the Acadian's engine and jumped out of the car. Bo's van was parked by the mouth of the alley.

As Swann sprinted for it, the Lincoln entered the alley and was brought up short by Swann's abandoned car that was blocking the exit. Swann gave them the finger as he reached the open side door of the van. Bo pulled away as he was getting in.

Bo turned left on Willard and booted the van up to Sunnyside where he took a sharp right. By the time they were on Riverdale, heading north for a connection with the Queensway which would take them to Eastway Gardens, they'd lost the Lincoln.

Swann climbed into the passenger's seat and tried to find room for his feet around Sooey's fat body.

"I love that move," Bo said. "Gets the suckers every time."

Swann nodded, grinning. "You give Jimmy the address?"

"Yeah. He'll meet us there with your car once the boys in the Lincoln take off."

Fifteen minutes later, they'd parked the van at the corner of Tremblay Road and Avenue "R" and were walking down the street to Bedard's house. Sooey watched them leave from the window of the van, but knew enough not to make a fuss. They checked out the neighbourhood as they walked, marking the houses, which had their lights on, which were dark. Bedard's was one of the latter.

They went up the short walk. Swann leaned on the bell while Bo ran a practiced eye over the lock.

"Great security," he said. "It's a Bird mortise and it's all yours, Jake."

Swann nodded.

While Bo shielded him from the street, he inserted first one pick, then a second into the keyhole. A few moments later the lock sprang open.

"Eighteen seconds," Bo said. "You're getting slow."

"Let's just get off the street, okay?"

"Touchy, touchy."

Swann opened the door and ushered Bo in. Wiping the knob, he stepped in behind. He took a pair of thin surgical gloves from his pocket and put them on, then locked the door behind them. Bo already had his gloves on and was prowling around, using a thin pencil flashlight to see by.

"I've repented," he said. "I've seen the fucking error of my ways. But Christ, I love this."

Swann could only shake his head. He moved to the living room window, stubbing his knee against a table. There were blinds on the window and he drew them shut.

"See if there's a light," he said.

Bo moved his hand along the wall near the door and found a switch. When he flicked it, a table light came on near the window.

The two men looked around the room. It looked like a doctor's waiting room. Four decrepit chairs stood against the walls, tables laden with magazines between each pair. Bo picked up one of the magazines. It was a glossy men's magazine with the subtle title of *Big Boobs*.

"Real cultural shit," he said as he threw it back down.

"Let's see if he's got an office."

They moved down a short hall. A door on the left opened up into a small bathroom that was also a darkroom. A chemical smell filled the air. The next room was furnished with a round waterbed and some gym floormats — the kind used for wrestling. Hanging from the walls were various leather masks, handcuffs, chains and other bondage paraphernalia. The room after that had a couch, a projection television set with a six foot screen and two video machines — one Beta and one VHS. The next room was set up like a traditional bedroom suite — double bed, dresser, two night tables. There were silk sheets on the bed, but nothing else. The last room, situated where the kitchen should have been, was the office they'd come looking for.

"Looks like we weren't the first," Bo said.

Swann nodded and they moved inside. The file drawers of the metal filing cabinet in one corner were all pulled open. Papers, magazines, files were strewn on the floor. A waist-high bookcase holding VHS and Beta cassettes ran along one wall. Half the cassettes were on the floor, the rest leaning against each other in disarray. There was a twenty-inch Sony Trinatron in a corner, video machines lined up beside it like a stereo shop display. The desk drawers had all been pulled and were piled beside the desk, their contents heaped on the floor beside them. The walls were covered with glossy black and white photographs of young men and women in various stages of undress.

Swann picked up a file and opened it.

The photo of a woman, head and shoulders shot, looked back at him. She appeared to be about eighteen, blonde, with large eyes and a wide mouth. There were more pictures of her in various poses that were supposed to be provocative, he realized, but just looked pathetic. An information sheet was included, taped to the back of the folder. It gave her name, address and phone number. Following that was a list of the various activities she was willing to partake in, running from traditional sex to progressively more disturbing acts.

He let the folder slip from his hand to fall to the floor.

"This shit's sick," Bo said.

He held up a photo to show Swann. It showed a pair of twins, a boy and a girl. They looked about eleven — twelve tops. He threw it aside.

"What're we looking for here, Jake? There's no way we're going to find a file on the Menzies girl in all this crap. Not unless we get real lucky."

Swann nodded. "See if you can find something on his clients. I'm going to check the basement."

"We gotta close this fucker down, Jake."

"We're working on it," Swann said.

The basement was finished and held what Swann assumed was the wardrobe department. Hundreds of outfits hung from a long rack that ran the length of the large room. There were spike heels, leather boots, rubber boots, and all types of footwear standing underneath the clothing rack. Even a pair of snowshoes. The other side of the room had two makeup tables with mirrors. Hanging from that wall were wigs of every style and colour and various animal masks. Dogs, lions, a rooster looked back at Swann.

A door leading off at the far end of the room opened into the furnace room. Another door led to where the video cameras and lights were stored. There was no paperwork.

Swann went back upstairs.

"I've got something," Bo said as Swann returned to the office.

He handed Swann some files. All of the kids in them were punks. Swann recognized Skiv, but none of the others. None of them was Trish Menzies.

"This it?" he asked.

Bo nodded. "All I could find. This operation's big, Jake. Look at the files. What did you find downstairs?"

"Clothing. Wigs. Cameras."

"We should burn this place down."

Swann shook his head. "We don't want to make the waves too big—not yet. Not until we find the Menzies girl."

"But what about all these other kids?"

"Let's handle it one thing at a time, Bo."

Swann moved over to the bookcase of videocassettes and started to look them over. They were in alphabetical order— the ones that remained on the shelves. It was mostly from the Js to the Rs that had ended up on the floor. The names used were first names only. Swann bent down to look for Trish under the Ts, but there was nothing there. He started to sift through the ones on the floor. Marcie #6. Julie #3 and #12. Mark #3. Then he found it.

Knickers #1.

He sifted through some more, found a Knickers #3, but that was it. No #2. No #4.

"Whatcha got there?" Bo asked.

Swann tossed him one, then crossed the room to the video machines. Both tapes were VHS. Files slid underfoot as he stepped on them and he kicked a path free through them. Turning on the TV, he inserted the cassette into a machine and hit the play button. Bo leaned on the desk and watched the screen with him.

This one had been taped inside the room with the waterbed. A thin girl was tied to the wall. She was naked, her features hidden by a leather mask that covered her head except for a hole for her mouth. A naked man stepped close to her, holding what looked like a whip with a corded silk end. He started to brush it along the girl's body.

Swann frowned and hit the fast forward. Images flickered by. They would have been comical, were it not for the subject matter. It wasn't until the counter on the video machine was up in the two thousands that the girl's mask was removed.

Swann hit the play button, then the pause. The screen froze on Trish Menzies' face. For a long moment the two men stared at the TV screen. Swann pushed the stop button and the screen dissolved into a dotted pattern. He removed the cassette and returned it to its case. Walter Menzies wasn't going to like this. Swann just felt sick.

"Are we gonna run him down now?" Bo asked quietly.

Swann nodded.

"What about all this shit in here?"

"We leave it—for now."

"How do you figure Rankin's connected?"

"He's covering their ass so far as the local cops are concerned. He's probably got partners in the OPP and with the Horsemen.

"And Sammy?"

Swann's knuckles went white around the cassette case.

"Sammy's where he made his big mistake," he said.

They left, taking the two videotapes with them, and found Swann's Acadian parked behind the van. Swann tossed the cassettes into the back seat of his car and peeled off his gloves.

"Did you have any trouble?" he asked Jimmy Crackle.

Jimmy was sitting on his haunches, leaning against the side of the van, smoking a cigarette. He shook his head.

"They burned a lot of rubber getting out of the lot, but they took too long getting onto Belmont. I waited until they were heading up Willard before I drove your car down to Billings and took Riverside to get here."

"They're gonna be waiting for you at your place," Bo said. "And they're not gonna be happy. They might do more than look this time."

"I doubt it."

"I think we should go back with you."

Swann shook his head.

"Why are you always so stubborn, Jevon?" Jimmy Crackle asked.

"They just want to know what we're doing," Swann replied. "Otherwise they'd have made a move before this."

"They made a move in the alley behind your place the other night."

"They were just flexing their muscles. They were seeing if I could be pushed, and I was showing them that I wouldn't be."

"So what do we do now?" Bo asked.

Swann glanced at his watch. It was just going on to eleven.

"We get some sleep. Then tomorrow we run down Bedard."

"You've got some ideas?"

Swann nodded. "I thought I'd go down to the Bourget Corporation's office and see about making a movie."

Bo and Jimmy Crackle exchanged glances.

"Either of you got a better idea?"

"I'll think on it," Bo said.

"Do that," Swann said. "Just remember, first I want the Menzies girl. I want her out of this. After that..."

He let the sentence hang there for them to fill in for themselves.

Bo smiled slowly. "Okay. After that, the shit hits the fan. C'mon, Jimmy. I'll drop you off. Where you going?"

"The Market will be fine."

"Thanks," Swann said. "We work well as a team."

"Just remember that," Bo said. "We are a team."

Swann nodded and got into the Acadian. When he coaxed it into life, he followed Bo's van as far as the Nicholas off-ramp on the Queensway. Bo turned off there. Swann honked and continued to the next exit at Metcalfe.

This time they were waiting for Swann inside his apartment.

He'd cruised slowly down Bank, not pulling into the alley behind his apartment until he was sure the street was clear. He left the Acadian in the alley and went up the fire escape. Inside, he switched on the light in the kitchen, got himself a beer and made his way to the living room. He took two steps inside when something hit him hard on the back of the head and he went down on the floor in a sprawl. The Budweiser can flew from his hand and landed by the window. The first thing Swann saw as the lights came on was the beer foaming from the can. Then he looked up.

He recognized the two men from the Lincoln. The one holding the .38 Police Special was about six-one, two hundred pounds squeezed into a dark suit, white shirt, no tie. His hair was dark and cut short above a squarish face. The one who'd hit Swann was still standing by the kitchen door. He was thinner, dirty blonde hair combed back from his forehead and parted on the left. He was wearing a suit as well, only his was a light brown, bagging at the knees and elbows. He had thin feral features that put Swann in mind of a weasel. In his hand was the small leather sap he'd used on Swann.

Swann assumed that these two had learned their lessons from the pair he'd taken out in the alley. They kept their distance. When Swann started to get up, the one with the gun shook his head.

"Uh-uh," he said.

Swann stayed on his hands and knees. From this position, with the gun trained on him, it would be impossible for him to make a play without getting shot.

"We heard about your moves," the gunman said. "Now it's time for you to learn about something."

"What's this all about?"

The gunman smiled. "If you have to be told, then we're wasting our time. But I think you know. What we want you to do is take a nice long vacation somewhere. Think you can do that?"

"Fuck you."

Swann had been watching the gunman. When the man with the sap came in from the side and kicked him in the stomach, he was totally unprepared for the blow. His breath left him with a whoosh of air and he could taste his dinner in his throat.

"Don't be stupid, Swann," the gunman said. "It's get burned, or take a nice vacation. We're even paying."

He took a handful of bills from his pocket and tossed them on the floor in front of Swann. They were all hundreds. There looked to be about fifteen hundred dollars lying there, all told.

"You...tell...You tell whoever you're working for that the only way I'm out of this is when I'm dead."

"We can arrange that, Swann. Christ, what's in this for you anyway? We know your rep. We all know you're a tough guy. So let's take a break from all this strutting around and get down to business. Take the bread. You need more, just ask. But take it. Get yourself a woman and go have a good time somewhere. When you get back, everything's going to be over and it's business as usual. It's either that, or..."

He let the word hang there, a look of mock regret in his eyes.

"Just saying I take it," Swann said. "What makes you think I'll stay gone?"

"Your word's supposed to be good, Swann. And besides. You come back and we'll blow you away."

"Maybe we better just get it over with right now," Swann said.

This time he could sense the man with the sap moving in. He watched the gunman's eyes, knowing they'd give his partner away. When something flickered in the gunman's gaze, Swann threw himself to his right. He hit the legs of the man with the sap, bowling him over. He had about three seconds, he figured, before the gunman would have a clear shot. He had to be on him in that time.

He came up off the floor in a rush, but already knew he was moving too slow. The man with the sap grabbed hold of his legs, the gunman started to squeeze the trigger of his .38, and then the eight-inch blade of a knife appeared in the gunman's wrist. He screamed, the gun falling to the floor with a clatter. Swann hit the man holding his legs, two quick blows to the nape of his neck, taking pleasure in each blow. Then he looked over to the kitchen door. Jimmy Crackle was moving towards the gunman. He drop-kicked the gunman, hitting him square in the chest, then crouched beside him as he fell and delivered a finishing blow.

Jimmy tore the man's shirt from his trousers and ripped most of the front of it away. Pulling out his knife, he wrapped the cloth around the gunman's hand, temporarily stanching the flow of the blood.

"You want the scalp?" he asked Swann, offering his knife.

Right at the moment, Swann wasn't sure if Jimmy was kidding or not. He shook his head. Jimmy shrugged, wiped the knife clean on the man's suit jacket, and slipped it back into the sheath on the inside of his right boot.

Swann's head was still ringing, but between the two of them they managed to manhandle the pair out the back and left them in the alley. Swann pocketed the sap. The .38 he stashed with the Magnum under his fire escape.

"Getting quite a collection there," Jimmy Crackle said.

Swann nodded. The movement made him dizzy. "I thought you were going home."

"I got lonely. Come on upstairs, Jevon. You've got blood on the back of your head. I want to have a look at it."

"I'm okay."

Except he was feeling woozy. All he needed right now was a concussion.

Jimmy Crackle had him lie on his stomach on his bed while he washed the wound out.

"How's your vision, Jevon?" he asked as he worked. "Are you seeing double, or are things blurry?"

"No. There's just a ringing."

Jimmy nodded. "You're going to have to take it a little slower for a couple of days, Jevon."

"Yeah, but—"

"Get some sleep. I'll be here."

"Sammy and Sue?"

"They're fine. Bo went to watch their place—just in case. You get some sleep now, Jevon. We'll talk in the morning."

Swann wanted to protest, but he just didn't have the energy. He lay on the bed, listening to Jimmy Crackle fix himself some tea in the kitchen. He heard Jimmy talking to someone on the phone and then he fell asleep.

Jimmy came in to look at him and covered him with a blanket when he saw that Swann was sleeping. He stood there for a few moments, listening to Swann breathe, then walked softly back into the kitchen. Opening the back door, he moved like a ghost down the fire escape. The blonde attacker was beginning to rouse as Jimmy approached him. When the blonde looked up, he found Jimmy crouched above him, the hunting knife in his hand.

"Don't come back," Jimmy said softly.

The blonde shook his head. "We're going, mister." He was still trying to work out how everything had gone so wrong, so fast. One minute he and his partner were in control, the next they were waking up in an alleyway with some Indian standing over them. "We're fucking gone."

"Good. I won't ask who sent you — I don't have to ask. Just tell him not to send anybody else, or *they*'ll be coming back in body bags."

He stood back and let the blonde man half-carry, half-drag his friend away and down the block to where they'd parked their car in somebody's driveway. Not until he could see their taillights disappearing into the distance did Jimmy return to Swann's apartment. He cleaned up the blood and the spilled beer from the hardwood floor in the living room. Counting the hundred dollar bills, he smiled as he laid them on the mantel. Maybe they'd help Jevon with his headache if he still had it in the morning.

When he had everything straightened up, Jimmy Crackle poured himself another cup of tea. Turning out the lights, he took the tea into the living room and sat with it by the window. He didn't need much sleep now — not as much as he used to when he was younger, and he'd never needed much. The rain that had fizzled out this morning returned. Jimmy Crackle sat and watched the glisten of the streetlights and store signs on the slick streets, smoking cigarettes and drinking tea until dawn.

Twenty-one

How are you feeling, Jevon?"

Swann blinked his eyes open to find Jimmy Crackle sitting on the edge of his bed with a coffee.

"Better," he said as he sat up. "Not great, but better."

He lifted a hand to gingerly touch the lump on the back of his head.

"It broke the skin, but I think you'll be all right. You've got a white man's hard head."

He handed the coffee to Swann who accepted it gratefully.

"Thanks."

"Sue called. You had a couple of messages."

"Christ, I never even heard the phone ring."

Jimmy Crackle smiled and held up the end of the phone plug.

"I thought you needed some sleep," he said as he plugged it back in. "I took the call on the kitchen phone."

"What time is it?"

"Ten."

Swann took a sip of his coffee. It was strong enough to stand a spoon in—just the way Jimmy liked it.

"Who were the messages from?" he asked.

"Lou Sweet was one."

"And the other?" Swann asked with a frown.

"A man named Steve Testa—he was calling for Danny Poirier."

"Now isn't that interesting?" Swann said as he reached for the phone.

"Something you should know," Jimmy Crackle said. "In case Lou brings it up. Bo broke into the Runaway—one of Poirier's restaurants—and trashed the place. Said he took exception to the way you'd been treated by the firm. Those are his words."

"Sounds more like what Poirier wants to talk to me about."

Jimmy shrugged. "I just thought you should know."

"Thanks. And thanks for last night, too."

"You're all I've got left to look after me in my old age," Jimmy said with a smile.

He was only half-joking, Swann knew. Jimmy took some of the old ways of his people very seriously, especially when it came to family units and respect for elders. Jimmy's trouble was he had no relatives left. The closest thing he had was Swann.

Swann reached for the phone again and decided to call Lou first. The anger started up in him again at Lou's cheerful hello.

"What's up?" he asked.

"We picked up the Buick. Thought I'd let you know, seeing how you were so interested yesterday."

"And?"

"It was clean. We found it abandoned out in Cyrville. Plates were gone. Registration numbers were filed to the metal."

"That's it?"

"You don't sound so shit-hot today, Swann. Are you all right?"

"I had a rough night. Listen, Lou. I've got to run. I'll talk to you soon."

He hung up and stared at the phone.

"Betrayal by a friend is the worst betrayal of all," Jimmy Crackle said.

Swann nodded. He picked up the phone again and dialed the number Jimmy had given him for Steve Testa. He didn't recognize the voice on the other end when the connection was made.

"Testa? This is Swann. What do you want?"

"Right to the point, eh? Well, Danny wants to talk to you, Swann. It seems we've got a problem."

"Only problem we've got is that you people are getting in my way."

"That's what Danny wants to talk to you about. You're getting the whole wrong idea, Swann."

"Those guys last night—are they part of the wrong idea I'm getting?"

"Something happened to you last night?"

"Let's not fuck around, Testa. What does Poirier want? If it's more of what his boys were offering last night, I'm still not interested."

"What are you on about, Swann?" Testa asked. "Danny didn't send anybody out to see you last night."

Swann stared at the wall of his bedroom. He tried to second-guess what Poirier hoped to gain by denying any involvement in what had happened to him last night, but couldn't come up with anything.

"You still there, Swann?"

"Yeah."

"Danny wants to set up a meet. How about we pick you up in half an hour?"

"No deal. He can meet me in the Avenue. I'll be at my usual table."

"Come on, Swann. Danny doesn't hit places like that anymore. He's got a rep to maintain."

"Well, then Danny isn't talking to me."

"Hang on a minute."

Swann worked at his coffee until Testa got back on the line.

"Danny says okay. We'll be there in half an hour. And, Swann?"

"Yeah?"

"Ask your friend the ox to lay off any more of our establishments until we get this talk out of the way, okay?"

"I didn't ask him to do anything."

"Yeah. Well, maybe you could ask him anyway."

"I'll see you in half an hour," Swann said and hung up.

Moving the phone to the night table, he looked over at Jimmy Crackle.

"Testa says those boys last night weren't Poirier's."

"That's interesting. You're meeting them downstairs."

"Yeah."

"I think I'll get myself a table with a nice view."

"I'm going for a shower," Swann said. "Then I'll give Sammy a quick buzz. I'll see you downstairs."

Jimmy left and Swann sat on the edge of his bed for a few moments longer, trying to puzzle it all out. At length he shrugged and padded into the bathroom for his shower.

No point in worrying at it. He'd find out what they had to say in twenty-five minutes.

Twenty two

Danny Poirier walked into the Avenue Restaurant wearing sunglasses and a light blue suit. A cream-coloured shirt was unbuttoned to show his chest hair and a half-dozen gold chains. His hair was dark and combed back from his forehead. He stood in the doorway, caught Swann's gaze and started for him after waving his bodyguard to a seat at the lunch counter. He walked with a swagger to his step.

Swann wondered if the bodyguard was Steve Testa. He was heavily built, with a weightlifter's shoulders. His sports jacket was tight across his back. His hair was short and dark, his features nondescript.

"Nice office you've got here, Swann," Poirier said.

He took out a handkerchief and gave the booth seat a cursory wipe before sitting down.

"Really classy."

"If you'd given me a little more time," Swann said, "I'd have sent out for some flowers."

Poirier smiled without humour. Removing his sunglasses, he put them in the breast pocket of his jacket. His eyes were a hard blue-grey.

"Let's get down to business," he said.

Swann leaned back. "It's your show for now — take the floor."

Poirier brought an envelope from the inside pocket of his jacket and laid it on the table between them. He covered it with his hand for a moment, then pushed it across the table.

"There's five bills in there," he said. "There'll be the same again when the job's done."

"That's a half-grand short of what you were offering me to get out of town last night."

"Let's stop fucking around," Poirier said. "I didn't offer you shit last night. I don't know anything about last night except that your pet ox trashed the Runaway. But I'm willing to forget that."

Swann looked down at the envelope. "So who do you want killed?"

"Are we going to do some business, or are we just going to sit here and bullshit?"

Swann pushed the envelope back into the centre of the table.

"Just what do you want, Poirier?"

"Look. I know we've had run-ins before, but we're basically operating on a leave-each-other-alone-policy — right?"

"Unless one of us steps out of line."

"You've got it. Well, a situation's come up where we can work together for a change."

Swann didn't say anything. He just waited for Poirier to get on with it.

"I want Marc Bedard," Poirier said. "I know you're looking for him and I don't care what you do with him once you've got him, but I want a chance to talk to him before you do anything with him."

"That's it?" Swann asked. "A grand — just to talk to some guy who already works for you? Come on, Danny. You can do better than that."

"How much do you want?"

Swann shook his head. "I'm not talking about more money. You tell me what you want with Bedard and I'll consider your offer."

"Where's this going? Just between you and me?"

"Depends."

"On what?"

Swann shrugged. "Maybe on what I hear now."

Poirier studied him for a long moment. "You're looking for a girl, right?"

Swann nodded.

"And that's it?"

Swann thought about Sammy and the rogue cop Rankin and Poirier's own accountant, but he didn't bring them up.

"First I'm looking for the girl," he said.

"You know the business Bedard was in?"

"We were out there last night. I've got a pretty good idea."

"Okay. Well, the thing of it is, we guarantee privacy. That comes first. Customer thinks you're going to fuck him and you're out of business."

"Some business."

"Come on, Swann. Don't go all prissy on me. The bimbos are begging to let us use them in these flicks. We're not forcing anybody to do anything they don't want to."

"Even kids that are eleven years old?"

"Where'd you hear that?" Poirier demanded. "We never use kids that young. Maybe they'll look that young, but every kid we use is over sixteen."

"Your business makes me want to puke, Danny."

"Not like yours, is it, Swann? All you do is dig through people's private lives and sell what you find. You're just a fucking white knight, aren't you?"

"Let's get back to your problem," Swann said.

"My problem's your problem, Swann. What it is, Bedard got greedy and started blackmailing some of our clients. One of them finally got wise and complained to me, but by the time I went looking for Bedard, he'd fucked off. So you see. You're looking for him, I'm looking for him."

"Are you saying he's left town?"

Poirier shook his head. "If he was smart, he would have left town. But Bedard's got a bee up his ass, Swann. He wants the whole pie now. What we've got is shaping up into a fucking gang war and I don't need it. It's shit on business. All it does is get people wired up. The press goes crazy. The cops need to come up with quick results. It plays fucking havoc on profits, Swann."

"So where do I come in?"

"Well, you see, when Bedard took off, he grabbed some of his juiciest flicks. We kept a copy of each one we made for our own leverage. With that in our hands, we didn't get hassled. But if he starts making them public, we've got nothing. I tell you, Swann, we had clients from all over the fucking country. Coming here. Just throwing their money in my pockets."

"In that dinky little studio?"

Poirier shrugged. "Keeps the overhead low. Besides, the clients like the seediness. I mean the whole thing's just a fucking game to them."

"So Bedard's in town and you want me to find him and bring him to you?"

"That's it. Him and the tapes. A grand all told. Half now — half on delivery."

"And what're you going to do with him?"

"All I want is my goods back, Swann. Without them, Bedard's got dick."

"I find it a little funny—you don't want his head for ripping you off?"

Poirier shook his head. "Where's the percentage in that, Swann? We got a pretty clean little city here. You see the homicide stats for last year? Nine. Nine stiffs for the whole year. If I start blowing people away and fucking up the cops' nice clean records, they're going to come gunning for me. I've only got so much pull. I keep a low profile, things are sweet. I fuck up too badly, and they bring me down."

He pushed the envelope back to Swann's side of the table. Swann stopped it and shook his head.

"I can't do it," he said. "I'm taking that business down."

"Bedard's got men on your ass, Swann. I don't. Let's stay friends. But Bedard...you've got to get him before he gets you."

"I'm not your friend, Danny."

Poirier studied him, a hard look in his eyes. "You don't want to be my enemy."

There was that, Swann thought.

"Look," Poirier said. "This business with underage kids is bothering you, right? Let me ask you this: I can find me a hundred twenty-year-olds that you'd swear were twelve. What do I want to fuck around with minors for? Nobody, and I mean nobody, is being forced to work for me, Swann."

"I saw pictures in Bedard's studio."

"What can I say? I'm telling you the way it is, Swann. I've got no reason to lie to you. I got enough men that one of them could take you out, but what do I want to do that for? I'm in business, Swann. Plain and simple. All I want is my cut. The percentages, without any hassles. Dealing with you's a hassle. Dealing with the cops is a hassle. I just don't need it."

Swann thought about it. He didn't need a war with Poirier either. There was absolutely no question that he'd get the short end of that stick.

"I didn't want any of your money," he said. "So what else can you do for me?"

"I'll owe you one."

Swann looked at him. In his mind he saw Poirier's accountant sitting around a table with Bob Rankin and Lou Sweet.

"I'll tell you what," he said. "I'm not making any promises, but I'll give you this: if I find Bedard before you do, the tapes he's got will disappear."

"That'll do."

"You might still lose that studio of Bedard's."

"Christ, Swann. You don't think we can put another together? We could operate this business out of a mobile van — which come to think of it, is not such a bad idea. It'd bring the overhead down. All we'd need is a vault for our copies of the tapes, just to keep the clients in line…"

He smiled at the look on Swann's face.

"You see," he said. "You just can't win, Swann. If people didn't want what we've got to sell them, we wouldn't exist. But all we're doing is providing a service. You could shut me right down. But all you'd get is a few months respite. I'd be back, or somebody else'd be in there faster than you could turn around. Trying to stop what we're doing is like pissing in the wind."

Swann pushed the envelope all the way over to Poirier's side of the table. Poirier pocketed it.

"The girl you're looking for," he said. "I'll bet you two-to-one she was in a flick with one of our VIP clients."

Swann remembered the missing Knickers #2 tape.

"I'm just starting to find out how weird Bedard was getting," Poirier continued. "If I was you, I'd chase him down as quick as possible. The only trouble is, you might not like what you find."

"What are you saying?"

Poirier stood up and put on his sunglasses. "I'm just guessing, Swann. Find Bedard. You get my tapes for me and the girl for yourself. And you'll still have me owing you one."

He lifted his hand jauntily and left Swann's table. Not until he was out of the restaurant, his bodyguard in tow, did Jimmy Crackle slide into the booth Poirier had so recently vacated. Swann filled him in.

"If Poirier can't find him," Jimmy said, "what makes him think you can?"

"I think he's got the feeling that I know where Bedard is."

He looked across the restaurant, a considering look in his eyes.

"And the funny thing is, I feel like I'm close to him myself."

"So where do we go now?"

"The Rideau Centre," Swann said. "I want to see if I can find a kid named Johnny — or maybe let him find me."

Twenty-three

Swann took a couple of slow tours through the ground floor of the Rideau Centre, especially taking his time in the food concession area where most of the teenagers seemed to hang out. He didn't spot Johnny, but he hoped Johnny had seen him. Guessing that the boy wouldn't want to be seen approaching him, Swann made his way back to the Nicholas Street entrance after awhile and leaned against the balustrade of the walkway leading down to the street.

He watched the pedestrians go by on Nicholas, admired the lines of the old courthouse. Just when he'd decided that he probably wouldn't be connecting with Johnny today, a skinny figure in T-shirt and jeans came out of the Centre and slouched against the wall beside him.

"I got the idea you were looking for me," Johnny said.

Swann nodded. "I had a couple more things I wanted to ask you."

"Shoot."

"When you made those films with Bedard, were they always in his studio in the East End?"

"What's this got to do with Knickers?"

"I find Bedard, I find her."

Johnny considered that.

"Makes sense," he said finally. "You've got to understand — I only did this a couple of times."

"I'm not here to make moral judgements," Swann said.

Though God knew he'd like to try. If Johnny was his son, he'd shake some sense into him. Then again, having a father lay down the law like that might be just what had sent Johnny into the streets in the first place. And like Johnny had said, you had to survive. But Swann didn't like it.

"Once it was with an old woman at the studio," Johnny said.

"How old?" Swann asked, startled. He hadn't considered women buying these cassettes.

"At least in her thirties."

"*That* old?" Swann said sarcastically.

Johnny gave him a grin. "Yeah. Your age, old man."

"What about the second time?"

"We went out to this place in the Gatineaus — a big estate off the Mountain Road. You can't see the place from the road for the trees, but you can't miss the entranceway. There's a couple of stone pillars — fieldstone, I guess — with lions on top of them. And lights."

"What kind of lights?"

"Like lanterns — you know?"

"Whose place was it?"

"I don't know. That time there were three of us. A girl named Josie — she works the Market, you know what I mean? — Sandy Sure and me. Bedard took us up in a van and we were there for the weekend. There were a few people floating around, but nobody talked much. All they wanted to do was get it on."

"You know anybody else that went up there?"

Johnny nodded. "A couple of the guys. Knickers was up once too. I think it was the second film she did."

Knicker's #2, Swann thought. Bingo.

"You up to taking me out there?" he asked.

"No way, man. But you can't miss the place. You know the road near Vanier that you can take to get up to Old Chelsea and Camp Fortune?"

Swann nodded.

"It's just before that. You won't miss it. I mean, how many places up there got lions guarding their lanes?"

"Okay," Swann said. "You've been a big help, Johnny."

"Well, let's just keep it between you and me, okay? Word gets around that I'm shooting off my mouth and I'm in deep shit."

"You got it. But I'll let you know how things turn out."

Johnny nodded and pushed away from the balustrade. The door to the Centre hissed shut behind him. Swann went back to where he'd parked his car behind the old police station. He repeated what he'd learned from Johnny to Jimmy Crackle, then went through it all again with Bo after he parked behind Bo's van on Waverley beside Sue's apartment.

"I think I know the place," Bo said. "Are we taking a spin out there now?"

"Later this afternoon. I want to get there just around dinnertime."

"What about Sammy and Sue?"

"We've got to expect that both Bedard and Poirier know about them and where they are. I don't like the idea of leaving them alone."

"I'll stay with them," Jimmy Crackle said. "I like that Sammy, Jevon. She's a good woman."

Swann sighed. "Are you going to play matchmaker now, too?"

"Man wants to be a fool and not see what's sitting right in front of his nose," Jimmy said, "who am I to tell him different?"

Bo grinned until Swann turned a frowning face towards him.

"So," he asked before Swann could say anything. "Are we going armed?"

Swann nodded. "I'm bringing a shotgun and we've got those handguns that our playmates left us."

"I think we should take the van," Bo said. "I'd hate like hell to have to trust your car if I wanted to get away from somewhere quick, Jake. Damn thing should have been junked years ago."

"It *was* junked," Jimmy Crackle said. "Where do you think Jevon got it?"

"Sure," Swann said. "Yuk it up, boys."

Jimmy Crackle flashed him a toothy grin, then his face went serious. "Poirier was willing to give us a bundle for free, Jevon. There's got to be more than his just wanting you to lead him to Bedard."

"Don't forget the tapes."

"I'm not. But I think he's trying to set you up."

"What for?" Bo asked.

"For whatever is going to happen to Marc Bedard," Jimmy said. "There's no way he's going to let Bedard get away with betraying him. He's going to let you take the fall, Jevon."

"That makes sense," Swann said. "It's just the way you'd expect Poirier to play it. He lets me go legging it after Bedard, making lots of waves so that everybody knows I'm after him, then when I do connect, he takes out Bedard and I'm standing there with my fly open."

Jimmy Crackle nodded. "He gets rid of an embarrassment and you — all at the same time."

"And he makes it stick," Bo added, "by having a few cops in his pocket."

"Well, it doesn't matter," Swann said. "The first priority is finding the Menzies girl — that's all we were hired to do." He paused, then added. "Anybody wants out, now'd be a good time."

Jimmy Crackle and Bo just looked at him.

"Okay. Then I guess we'll have to see which way things fall and play it by ear."

"Just so long as they don't fall on us," Bo said.

"We'll have to stay on our toes," Swann said. "That's all. Now I'm going to spend some time with Sammy. How about if we leave here around six?"

"Want us to pick up the guns from your place?"

Swann nodded. "You might want to stay out of Poirier's restaurants for the next couple of days, Bo."

Bo gave him an innocent look. Swann just shook his head and left them on the pavement while he went inside to Sue's apartment.

Twenty-four

Swann spent the remainder of the afternoon with Sammy and Sue. They played some music for him that left him with the familiar feeling of wishing he could play an instrument himself. Sue's timing was a little off on the fiddle tunes — Celtic music depended on a certain feel for the music, a lift, as much as its strict tempo — but she shone on the classical pieces. Sammy's fiddling was precise as they played through a simple Albinoni concerto, impressing Swann again with just how good she was. It made him wonder that she never went beyond playing on the street and in small clubs, augmenting that meager income by giving fiddle lessons both at home and through the Ottawa Folklore Centre.

Afterwards, Sammy and Swann sat on the steps outside Sue's apartment, watching the traffic go by on Elgin. It was rush hour and the street was clogged with cars and buses. Cyclists sped past the slow moving traffic and the sidewalk was busy with pedestrians, mostly the young upwardly mobile executive types that had taken over the area, though there was a fair sprinkling of people from other walks of life.

"I saw Bo's van parked on Waverley most of the night," Sammy said. "It was there when I had to get up for a pee in the middle of the night and it was still there when you showed up today. What's going on, Jake?"

"Nothing much. Better safe than sorry, that's what I always say."

"Now you're scaring me. You think those guys are going to track me down again?"

Swann shook his head. "No. It's just my own paranoia. It's got to do with a case I'm working on."

He gave her a quick rundown on recent events, leaving out anything to do with Rankin or Lou Sweet. He didn't fool her for a minute.

"You're not telling me everything, Jake. You're chasing down those guys that attacked me—aren't you?"

"Well, I'm looking into it—just on the side."

"I want to know what you've found out. I want to be a part of this."

"Come on, Sammy..."

"No, you come on, Jake. I'm the one that ended up in the hospital. Sue was telling me about what happened to her, you know, and the thing she said that made the most sense is that people have got to stop thinking of themselves as victims. When your mind's in that kind of set, you're already half-beaten. That's what happened to her, but it's not going to happen to me."

"Are you talking about vigilantism?"

"Isn't that what you're planning?"

"I don't know what I'm planning yet, Sammy. Everything's gotten a lot more complicated than it was when I started. Remember what I said about revenge."

"I've thought about it—I've fantasized about it, Jake. Maybe it doesn't solve anything, but maybe it'll stop it from happening to someone else. And I've got the feeling that it'll make me feel a whole lot better."

Swann turned to look at her. The swelling was down in her face, but the bruises still blotched her skin. She didn't look good. Walking was still painful. And inside....What she felt inside had to hurt a lot more than the anger burning in himself.

"I don't know," he said.

"Listen, Jake. I really appreciate all you've done for me. Really. I mean, no one else came, but you were there. You didn't ask for anything, you were just there. Now maybe I've been putting some pressure on you, maybe you'd like our relationship to stay just the way it's been—I don't know, you haven't said a whole lot to me about it. But we're still friends, no matter what, right?"

"Sure."

"Well, friends stand by each other, Jake. Even when they make mistakes."

"You could get hurt—maybe worse than you already have been—by making this mistake," Swann said.

Sammy shook her head. "Nothing could hurt me worse than the way I felt on Friday night, Jake. *Nothing.* I've been low before, but that night I was scraping the bottom. God! I still feel nervous just being outside—even sitting here with you. What if that feeling doesn't leave me? I've got to see these guys get what's coming to them, Jake. Otherwise I'm going to be scared of them for the rest of my life.

"You know, in the hospital, I didn't even want the doctor to come near me—just because he was a man. When I first saw Jimmy sitting there beside my bed, I almost died, I was so uptight. Even being with you makes me a little nervous—and I *know*, heart and soul, that you'd never hurt me. Don't you think those bastards deserve to pay for what they've done to me?"

Swann nodded slowly. "They'll pay."

"Don't close me out of this, Jake," she said. She laid a hand on his arm. "Please. Talk to me about it."

So he told her. What he knew. What he guessed about the connection between Rankin and Poirier. Everything.

"Not Lou," she said.

She'd met Lou Sweet once and heard Swann talk about him a lot.

"He was there," Swann said. "He was at Rankin's when he said he didn't know him."

"He wasn't one of the men...who...he wasn't there that night, Jake. I would have recognized him."

"Maybe he wasn't. But he's connected to Rankin. And Poirier."

"What are we going to do, Jake?"

"I don't know. Bo and I are going out to that place on the Mountain Road tonight. I guess we'll just have to play it by ear."

"And this Rankin?"

"I can't touch him until I find out what happened to the Menzies girl. After that he's fair game."

"You'll tell me before you do anything?"

Swann nodded. They sat quietly for a few moments, watching the thinning traffic.

"Guess I'm getting a little pushy," Sammy said suddenly.

"No. You're okay, Sammy."

"About you and me, I mean."

Swann smiled briefly. Everyone had their own ideas about how things should work out between them.

"Let's not jump into anything," he said. "I like you an awful lot, Sammy. When I first met you, I wanted you, but then we became friends and I guess I just didn't want to mess that up."

"Lovers should be friends, too."

"I've never had much luck with relationships," Swann said. "Christ knows, you've heard me talk about them often enough."

"You just never had the right partner."

Before Swann could say anything, she laid a finger across his lips.

"I know," she said. "Now's not a good time to get into any of this. But think about it, Jake."

"I've been doing a lot of thinking about it — last couple of days."

A car horn honked, interrupting any further conversation. They looked up to see Bo's Econoline parked at the curb. Sooey was in the passenger's seat, staring out at them. Jimmy Crackle stepped out of the side door.

"Saved by the bell," Sammy said. "I know you, Jake. You don't like to commit yourself because you've been burned too many times before. Well, I've been there, too. But we've got one thing going for us now."

"What's that?"

Sammy smiled. "We already know each other." She leaned a little closer to him. "You take care now, Jake."

"I will."

He got up when Jimmy Crackle reached them.

"Ready to go, Jevon?" Jimmy asked.

Swann nodded. "I'll see you guys later."

Jimmy Crackle and Sammy watched him get into the van, watched the van until it was lost from sight behind a bus.

"Well, I've got to run," Jimmy said. "Be seeing you, Sammy."

"Jake's told me everything," Sammy said, "so you might as well come inside and be comfortable, Jimmy." She shook her head. "You guys."

Jimmy Crackle grinned and followed her into Sue's apartment.

Twenty-five *ᒪ o Chapter*

Due to the Québec Language Bill 101, which flagrantly ignored the federal mandate making Canada a bilingual country, all of Québec's road signs were in French only. This didn't present a problem for Bo, who spoke both languages, but it always left Swann feeling as though he'd entered a foreign country as soon as he crossed the river that separated Québec from Ontario. Instead of turning off Boulevard Alexander Taché onto what was previously called the Mountain Road, they turned onto Chemin de la Montagne. Swann had always preferred the English version because it bore the same name as one of his favorite Irish reels.

"So you filled her in," Bo said.

Swann nodded.

"And she wants to be there when we bring him down?"

"Yeah."

"Can't say's I blame her. I'd say it was her right, Jake."

"I just don't like the idea of her getting caught up in all this."

"I don't think she had a whole lotta choice."

"But she's not prepared for this kind of a situation."

"We're not in such shit-hot shape ourselves, Jake. It's been a couple of years since we've had to get down and get funky. You think we're getting soft?"

Swann thought about the way he'd handled himself in the alley, then remembered how he'd gotten suckered in his own apartment the next night.

"We've been in better shape," he said.

"And guns just make you sloppy."

Swann nodded. Bo had kept the Magnum for himself, giving Swann the .38. The shotgun lay on the floor between their seats, covered with a blanket.

"We need an edge," he said.

Bo nodded. "But guns aren't it. Not when they're gonna have more."

He started to slow down as they neared the area where Johnny had told Swann the estate lay. Swann spotted it first.

"Keep going," he said as Bo started to slow down.

Bo took his foot off the brake and they cruised by. Johnny had been right, Swann thought. There was no way you could miss the place. The lions were of grey stone and crouched on top of two square pillars. Ornate lanterns, heavy on the brass, rose behind them. Between the pillars he caught a glimpse of a lane leading up the side of the mountain, but whatever it led to was hidden by the heavy tree cover.

"You see anything?" Bo asked.

Swann shook his head. "But if this place is what I think it is, there'll be guards. Not ones we can spot from the road, but they'll be there all the same."

"Gotcha."

He drove another half mile. They passed the turnoff to Old Chelsea and the Camp Fortune ski slopes and Bo pulled the van into the dirt parking lot of a restaurant/general store at the corner of Chemin de la Montagne and Boulevard Vanier. He parked under a large shady maple and killed the engine. The store was the first building they'd seen since passing the entrance to the estate. South of them were unkempt farmers' fields. North, coming right down to the road, were the foothills of the Gatineau Mountains.

"Are we taking the shotgun?" Bo asked.

Swann nodded. The shotgun was a pistol grip TP-8 police and survival pump shotgun made in Italy that held eight cartridges. Slipping it under his jacket, he stepped from the van, moving stiffly to keep the gun out of sight. Bo locked up and joined him on the dirt parking lot. Sooey rushed around the lot, sniffing at everything until Bo called the dog to him. They started down the road then, taking to the bush as soon as the restaurant was hidden by the trees.

"Just like old times," Bo said. "Remember that field of dope we had back then? Course, that was before you went straight on me."

Swann smiled. "I had to stop smoking. It just got to the point where I'd either fall asleep or get sick, Bo. What can I say?"

"That says it all, Jake. You just wimped out on me is all. You know, we should have brought the Indian with us. This is right up his alley."

"Why do you always call him that?"

"I like the way it makes you frown. Heads up."

Sooey had paused ahead of them. Swann shifted the shotgun so that his right hand was around the pistol grip. He held the barrel with his left. The two men hunched down beside the bull terrier and studied the open ground between themselves and the stone building of the estate. The house rose two floors and looked to have at least ten or twelve rooms. The lawns were well tended and dotted with sculpted cedars and pines. Lilacs, just losing their lavender blooms, leaned up against the fieldstone walls of the house that faced them.

"I don't see any guards," Bo said.

"Maybe they're just down by the gates."

Bo shrugged. "So who do you think owns this place?"

"I'm betting it belongs to Weppler—the accountant. Him or Sigouin. Can't be Bedard's. Poirier would have already checked it out if it was."

"Who's to say he hasn't?"

Swann frowned. "You got any better ideas?"

"You're the boss, Jake — God help us. How do you want to work this?"

"Direct approach. I'll take the front, you take the back. We'll just go in and get ourselves some answers."

"Great plan. You think it up all on your own?"

"Let's go."

Swann stepped from the trees and trotted for the front door, the shotgun held up against his chest under his coat. He got to the corner of the house when he heard a rifle crack. A bullet hit the wall near his shoulder, ricocheting from the stone with a whine. Swann dropped to the ground as a second bullet hit the building right where he'd been standing.

He didn't check where they were coming from. There wasn't time. He came up in a roll, a third bullet whining by his ear, and sprinted for the door. He didn't bother with any finesse when he reached it. He just pumped a shell in place and blew the lock out, then kicked the door in. Another bullet smashed into the doorjamb as he went in, spitting splinters.

There was a man standing in the hallway, reaching under his jacket for a gun. Swann shook his head, but the man ignored him. Holding the shotgun like a bat, Swann moved in and swatted the man alongside the head with the barrel just as he was bringing his gun free. The man dropped, his gun hitting the floor a moment before he did himself. Swann scooped up the weapon and, with it in his left hand, the shotgun in his right, started up the stairs.

He could heard a commotion around the back of the house as he went up. Jesus, he thought. They were playing this all wrong. He kicked in the first door at the top of the stairs. It was an empty bedroom. He was moving towards the next when he caught a glimpse of movement further down the hall.

"Hold it!" he cried.

There was a man there holding a gun in one hand, a briefcase in the other. As he started to bring the gun up, Swann fired the .38 he'd taken from the man downstairs. He shot deliberately high.

"The next one goes through you," he warned.

The man dropped his gun on the floor where it fell with a muffled clatter on the carpet.

"Nice and easy now," Swann said. "Move towards me."

The man looked scared, which suited Swann just fine. He was thin, well-dressed in dark trousers and a light sportsjacket. His hair had what was probably a perm, swept back from the brow, and his eyes were small. He had almost no chin. He was visibly trembling as he moved towards Swann.

"Who—who sent you?"

"Nobody sent me."

Swann thrust the handgun behind his belt and, holding the shotgun with both hands, he moved around the man until he could pick up the weapon his captive had dropped. He was acquiring quite an arsenal.

"You Bedard?" he asked as he straightened up.

Bedard nodded.

"How many men have you got here?"

"Four. Listen. If Danny sent you—I can top whatever he offered."

"I told you—I'm here by myself. Where are your guards?"

"One outside and three downstairs."

"Hey, Jake!" Bo bellowed from the lower floor. "You okay?"

"Yeah," Swann called back.

"Come on," he told Bedard. "Let's go downstairs."

"You're Swann?" Bedard asked. "Listen, I can—"

"Downstairs."

When they reached the top of the stairs, Swann found Bo waiting for him in the foyer below. He had two men with him, lined up against the wall beside the man Swann had taken out. Sooey stood guard over them. One of the men standing gripped his arm where his jacket hung in tatters. Sooey had done his bit, Swann thought. The other was the blonde-haired man that had been in Swann's apartment.

"Things got a little messy," Bo explained.

"I can see that. There's still one outside."

Swann hauled Bedard up to the door and put the shotgun against the back of his head.

"Call him off," he said. "I want him in here, unarmed, or you lose your head."

"Oh, Jesus. Come on. I can—"

"Call him!"

"Jerry!" Bedard cried, his voice going a little shrill. "Fercrissakes, Jerry. Don't shoot anymore!"

Swann was watching over Bedard's shoulder. "Tell him to get in here."

Bedard called out the order and a long moment passed. Then a figure stepped from the trees by the lane coming up from Chemin de la Montagne. He was holding a rifle. He walked towards the house, the barrel pointing at the ground.

"Tell him to drop that rifle. And if he's packing, I want that on the grass, too."

He nudged the back of Bedard's head with the barrels of the shotgun and Bedard stuttered out the order.

The man, seeing how things were, laid down the rifle. He pulled a handgun from a belt holster and laid it beside the rifle, then walked towards the house with his hands in the air.

"Your plan worked real good," Bo said.

Swann glanced at him. Bo was grinning, but there was worry in his eyes. Swann nodded. This had been just a little too close. They really had gone soft.

He pulled Bedard from the door as the rifleman came in and motioned for him to join the three men Sooey was guarding.

"What're we going to do with 'em?" Bo asked.

"Blondie might be a problem," Swann said. "He was at my place that night—he's the one that sapped me."

"Hey, I'm not going to be any problem at all," the blonde-haired man said. "You've got the man who pays our way. Without him, we're not working for anybody. You say blow, and we blow."

Swann glanced at Bedard. "There a place in here where we can lock them up while we talk?"

"Down-downstairs. In the basement."

"Let's go, boys," Bo said. "Lead the way."

He took over holding Bedard, letting Swann cover the men. The shotgun had a wider spread and the men were more afraid of it than the Magnum Bo held. But they were all afraid of Sooey — especially the one that had gotten his arm chewed up. Swann let Sooey shepherd them into the basement.

There was more movie-making equipment downstairs, both video and 16mm film. Bedard pointed out a windowless storage space and Swann crowded the four bodyguards into it. There was a padlock on the outside that he hooked into place once the men were inside and he had the door closed. The lock snapped shut with click.

"Who owns this place?" Swann asked, turning back to Bedard.

"Guy named Howland. Don Howland."

Swann and Bo exchanged glances. The name didn't ring any bells.

"Let's go upstairs," Swann said, "and have ourselves a friendly chat."

Twenty-six

They sat Bedard down at a table in the kitchen. Swann sat opposite him while Bo drifted from the front to the back of the house, keeping an eye out for possible trouble. Sooey settled at Swann's feet. The kitchen was big enough to fit most of Swann's apartment into it.

"There was no way I could keep Danny out of my business," Bedard said. "He decided to expand from just dealing dope, you see, and the porn business looked good, what with the boom in home video equipment and Ontario's censorship laws. And you're always going to find people who want a little something extra—something personal."

"Like the films you provide."

Bedard nodded. "It's just supply and demand. Simple stuff."

Swann heard an echo of Poirier in Bedard's voice. Why was it that once criminals got organized, they were always trying to justify themselves?

"How much money can there be in this business of yours?" he asked.

"Well, it started small, you know. Just a sideline. But the kind of service we provide—word of mouth got around and now we're dealing with people all over North America. That's where Danny really came in—he's got the connections to really take it someplace big."

Swann nodded. "And he provides you with protection from the law?"

"Sure. Protection from anybody else wanting to cash in on the thing we've got going."

"So what happened? The perfect relationship developed some flaws?"

"That's an understatement."

"And Howland. Who's he? Where does he fit in?"

"When Danny first approached me, I didn't want him to own me, but I didn't have any upfront money either. It was never a question of saying no. I knew Danny had to have a slice if I wanted to survive, but I figured if I put up some bread too, he wouldn't just walk all over me. So what I needed was a silent partner and that's where Howland stepped in."

"So you end up having two guys own you."

"Howland's not like that," Bedard said. "We've got a sweet deal — sweet for him and me. He gets sixty; I get forty. The percentages might not sound so great, but we're talking some real money here."

"Where's Howland now?"

"Out of the country on a business trip."

Swann nodded. Just waiting for it all to blow over, he thought.

"So what's the story between you and Poirier?" he asked.

"Something fucked up. Danny fucked up. He got greedy and started coming back to some of the clients with copies of the tapes — wanting a little extra bread. A couple of them wouldn't give, they called down the law, and suddenly Danny's got a real problem. Cops he's got in his pocket can't do a thing, so Danny decides to let me take the fall for it all."

The old domino theory, Swann thought.

"Poirier says it was you that got greedy."

"That's bullshit."

"Well, where are the tapes — the ones that were being used for blackmailing?"

Bedard looked nervous. "I've got them. But you see, we made more than one dupe. Everybody important, Danny got a copy of their little show."

"Somebody trashed your studio in Eastway Gardens."

"I haven't been out there for a couple of weeks."

"What do you think they were looking for?"

"Tapes—what else?"

"Any idea who it was?"

Bedard shook his head. "Danny, maybe. Maybe one of our clients."

"What about this place?" Swann asked. "I heard you made some films out here."

"Some clients like a nicer place. And then some of Howland's friends like to get it on—but in private, you know? I'd do that from time to time. Take a couple of cameras, pick up a few kids and head out to wherever they wanted. Usually we came here. Fuck it, it's their money. I charged triple for those trips."

"Howland ever get into it?"

"That's how he came to be my partner. I was running a straight business—ads, that kind of shit—when he asked if I could do him up something special. The whole thing was his idea, really."

"Who's got the tapes with him on them? Poirier?"

"Danny doesn't know. The only copies of those tapes are here."

Swann shook his head. "I don't buy that, Bedard."

He was thinking about the wall of videocassettes he'd seen in Bedard's office. The Knickers #2 was missing and Johnny had told him that her second filming had taken place up here. If there hadn't been copies of the estate films at the office, the numbering system would have been different.

"Come on, Swann," Bedard said. "What am I going to lie to you for?"

Swann pulled the photos of the Menzies girl from his pocket and laid them down in front of Bedard.

"Do you know her?"

Bedard licked his lips nervously. "Sure. Sure, I know her. Calls herself Knickers."

"Where's the tape labeled #2?"

"Must be back at the studio—"

"One and three are there, but no #2."

"I guess somebody must have ripped it off."

"It was filmed up here," Swann said.

He reached over and pulled the briefcase from beside Bedard's chair. Bedard started to complain, but Sooey lifted his head and growled. Bedard sat back in his chair, looking like he wanted to bolt. Swann expected the case to be locked, but it snapped open on his first try. Inside were a number of videocassettes, some paperwork, and what looked to be a lot of money in twenties, fifties and hundreds. One of the cassettes was labeled "Knickers #2."

"This got Howland on it?"

Bedard nodded.

"What were you planning to do with it?"

"When...when Howland saw the way things were going, he was all set to let me take the fall—just like Danny. I had nothing on him—nothing signed, you understand? Between him and Danny I was set up to do a lot of time—if I even lived long enough to get my day in court."

"They were working together?"

"No. But they were hitting me from both sides. I needed some leverage against Howland."

Swann snapped the briefcase shut. "Here's where it gets simple," he said. "I'm keeping the tapes—all of them. You can have your money back, but first you tell me what happened to the girl."

"The girl?" Bedard looked visibly astounded. "What do you mean the girl?"

"Where is she?"

"Christ, how should I know? She's just some punkette, fercrissakes. Do you think I keep tabs on those kids? When I need one, I just cruise a couple of areas where I know they'll be hanging out. When it's over, I pay them off and drop them back where I found them. I don't know dick about them. And they don't know anything about who their co-stars are, you know?"

"Find her and get her back to me," Swann said, "or you lose on all sides. You lose the money, Howland washes his hands of you, and Poirier lets you take the fall. Bring her to me and at least you've got the money. You can take off—use the money for a stake. I can't figure out why you didn't just do that in the first place."

"I was trying to work things out, Swann. Where am I going to go? Danny's got connections everywhere."

"I don't really give a shit," Swann said. "All I want is the girl."

"I swear to you, Swann. I don't have her. Christ, she could be anywhere. You give those kids a bit of bread and they either blow it on drugs or they fuck off with it."

Swann sighed. "That's too bad for you."

He stood up and hefted the briefcase.

"I'm stashing this someplace, Bedard, so don't get any funny ideas about sending your goons out after me. Anything happens to me, and you'll never get your money back. You following me so far?"

Bedard gave him a nervous nod.

"Though you'd think after sending them around twice, you would've learned by now that you weren't getting rid of me so easily."

"Twice? I only sent a couple of guys last night."

"What about the two men in the Buick? The ones I put in the hospital? The ones that knocked off Cohen?"

"I had nothing to do with that," Bedard said. "I swear. I sent a couple of guys, sure. The deal was to get you out of town until I could maybe work something out with Danny and Howland. I didn't know what you were looking for, just that you were getting to be a pain. I thought this shit about Knickers

was just a front. Anyway, you put one of them in the hospital —
or at least your Indian friend did — and you saw Paulie here.
He's the blonde guy you locked up with the others downstairs."

Swann studied him for a long moment. He tended to believe
him, on this at least.

"Who does Poirier have in his pocket?" he asked suddenly.
"Give me some names."

"I don't know, Swann. You'd have to ask Danny. I never
dealt with them. Christ, if I had names, I'd try to run a deal
through with them."

Swann nodded. He believed him on this as well.

"The Menzies girl," he said. "Knickers. I want to know
where she is. When she's safe, I'll let you know where I've
stashed your money."

"Jesus, Swann. I already told you..."

"The girl," he said and he left the room, Sooey at his heels.
He met Bo out by the front door.

"I got a car to take us down to the van," Bo said, "and I've
fixed the other two so they can't follow us. You get what you
want?"

"Just another piece to the puzzle," Swann said. "Come on.
I'll fill you in on the way home."

"Sure. Hey, Jake. You should've seen Sooey tear into them.
The damn dog's got balls. I always told you that, but do you
ever pay any attention to what I'm saying..."

Twenty-seven

They left the borrowed car in the lot where they had parked the van, taking its distributor cap with them. Bo laid his Magnum on the blanket between their seats when they got into the van. Swann put his handguns and the shotgun there, then covered them all over with a fold of the blanket.

"Now what?" Bo asked.

"Looks like we've got to pay a call on Poirier," Swann said.

Bo gave him a quick hard look. "Back there—about the only thing that let us pull that off was pure shit-blind luck, Jake. That's not gonna happen again."

"I know. But Poirier likes to talk and that's all we're going to do."

"We gonna see him now?"

"No. I've got a couple of things to check into first."

"Like what?"

"Bedard's studio, for one."

"You figure we missed something?"

"If not there, then somewhere along the line. Things just aren't hanging together, Bo. All we're doing is getting more and more caught up in this bullshit between Poirier and Bedard, with nothing on the girl."

"Not to mention this other business with Rankin."

Swann nodded. "But I've got a feeling, Bo, that everything's part of the same puzzle."

"Even what happened to Sammy?"

"Like I said before, that's where somebody made their big mistake."

———

There was a car parked in the lane of Bedard's studio when they drove down Avenue "R." Bo glanced at Swann, but before he could ask, Swann told him to drive on.

"This is a dead end, Jake."

"Yeah. And that was Lou Sweet's car. Turn around and drop me off, then head on back to Tremblay. Wait for me on the next road over. I want to have a peek in the window and see what he's up to."

Bo didn't like it, but he drove the van to the end of the avenue and let Swann off.

"You be careful," he said.

Swann nodded. He waited until Bo had reached Tremblay, then slowly made his way up the street. As he neared Bedard's place, he slipped into the neighbour's yard and eased his way closer to the studio. There were no lights on that he could see, or at least no light coming through any of the windows. Then he remembered what it was like inside. The kind of gigs Bedard did, he didn't want any Peeping Toms.

Swann was just trying to decide whether he should go in and confront Lou, when he heard the front door open. He padded quickly to the front of the house and had a brief look around the corner. He recognized Lou. With him was Poirier's accountant, Keith Weppler.

"—makes sense," Weppler was saying. "I was by on the weekend and everything looked okay."

"And now it's all gone," Lou said. "This is not going to look good. Without those…"

Swann lost the rest of the conversation as the two men got into Lou's car. He stayed where he was until their taillights were turning off onto Tremblay Road, then moved for the front door. It was unlocked, so he put away his picks and stepped inside. He walked down the dark hallway and flicked on the light in the office.

Now he understood what Lou and the accountant had been talking about. The office had been cleaned out. Videos, files, it was all gone.

He circled slowly around the office, double-checking, then left the studio and walked to the next street where Bo was sitting in the van, impatiently tapping his fingers against the steering wheel.

"Everything's gone," Swann said as he slid into the passenger's seat.

"Lou took it?"

Swann shook his head. "No. They seemed surprised as well."

Bo started up the van. "Where to now?"

"Why don't you drop me off at Cooper Street and we'll call it a night."

Bo turned the van in a laneway and took them back downtown via the Queensway.

"You want me to wait for you?" he asked as he pulled up at the corner of Cooper and Kent. "It's a long trot back to Sue's place."

"I don't know how long I'm going to be."

"I got nothing else on."

"Okay."

Bo parked on Cooper and killed the engine. Swann gave Sooey a quick pat, then started down the street to where the party had been the other night. The house wasn't lit up like it had been that night, but loud music was still spilling out onto the street and the girl was in her spot by the door, smoking a joint. She looked warily at Swann, then recognized him.

"Skiv around?" he asked.

"He's inside. Hey, listen. You've got some more questions, why don't you ask me this time? I could use the bread."

"Maybe some other time," Swann said.

He stepped by her and went in through the open door. There was a long hallway leading to a kitchen at the far end. The music came from a room to his right. Three young punks sat on a battered couch with a couple of band posters tacked to the wall behind it. One showed Becki Bondage from Vice Squad, in her usual leather and chains. The other was a "Holidays in the Sun" Sex Pistols poster. The stereo sat on a couple of apple crates, the speakers in each corner of the room. A milk crate half full of records stood in front of the stereo. Singles and LP jackets lay in scattered piles to either side. Swann didn't recognize the music. All he knew was that it was loud and the band was making up in enthusiasm for what they didn't know about playing instruments.

The punks ignored him until he came into the room and asked for Skiv. He had to repeat himself over the music. The smell of marijuana smoke was strong in the air. The punks were sharing a quart of Ex.

"He's in the kitchen," one of them replied.

Swann nodded his thanks and went down the hall. He found Skiv sitting at the rickety kitchen table. The sink looked as though it had about a week's worth of dishes in it. A blonde girl was sitting on Skiv's lap—her hair right out of a bottle of peroxide. She looked about fourteen.

"M'man," Skiv said.

"Can we talk?" Swann asked.

"Sure. But I'm not in the mood for a walk. Pull up a chair, Mr. Private Eye, and slap your wallet on the table."

"Maybe there's not so much money in this."

"Then maybe I don't have a whole lot to say."

"I'm looking for a guy named Johnny. He wears his hair in a Mohawk and has a silver bomb earring hanging from his ear. He's maybe seventeen, eighteen. Skinny. Hangs out around the Rideau Centre."

"I know him. Johnny Thurston. What about him?"

"What's the story on him?"

"He knew Knickers, if that's what you're getting at."

"Yeah. I know that. What I'm wondering is, what's his connection with Marc Bedard?"

Skiv studied him for a moment, then he pushed the girl off his lap and gave her a slap on the rump.

"Fuck off for awhile, Jess."

He waited until she'd left the kitchen before looking back at Swann.

"I heard about Cohen," he said.

"What are you getting at?"

"So this is going to cost you."

"How much?"

"A hundred."

Swann shook his head. "Forty—same as before. Take a lesson from Cohen, if you want to stay in business. Keep your prices reasonable and you'll get a lot more repeat trade."

"Cohen is *dead,* man. What kind of fucking lesson's that? I'll tell *you* what. You got to get what you can and stay off the streets, man."

Swann took out a pair of twenties and a ten and laid them on the table.

"Let's hear what you've got to say."

Skiv stared at the money for a long moment, then scooped up the bills and stuffed them into a pocket of his jeans.

"Johnny had a kid brother—we all called him Grubber. He used to have this gig picking worms on a golf course—grubbing, get it?"

"I get it. What happened to him?"

"He ODed. Happened at Bedard's place one night. Bedard provided the skag. Johnny took it a little hard. Blamed Bedard, but what the fuck. Nobody made the kid take anything."

"You were there?"

Skiv nodded. "Sure. I took a hit myself. Didn't fuck me up one bit. Course the thing with me and drugs is that I'm so naturally fucked up they just sort of level me out to a normal state."

"How old was the kid?"

"Fourteen."

"I heard Bedard doesn't use kids under sixteen."

"Well, he tries to, but come on, man. He's not going to start asking for ID."

Swann nodded. "You're the guy that steers the kids to Bedard?"

"Yeah. I get a little cut for every fresh butt I sent over. Guy needs to make a buck."

"And it's mostly just the punks?"

Skiv laughed. "Shit, no. Most of 'em wouldn't go near a gig like that. But you get 'em a little high and sometimes things work out. And after the first time, they see it's no big deal. They come back when they need the bread."

"Johnny got anything against you — for what happened to his brother?"

"No way, man. Maybe I talked the kid into going — but it was Bedard fed him the shit. I think maybe he just couldn't cut it, you know? Some people are like that."

"Bedard says he doesn't know where Knickers is."

"Well, who does?"

"He says she got paid off and probably just took the money and ran with it."

"A lot of 'em do that. Or they get themselves a place, go straight — job, the whole scene. There's not a whole lot of hardcore left, man. Not like it used to be."

"Where do you think she is?"

"Well, if she's out of the city, you could try T.O. Or even Vancouver."

"You have reasons for thinking that?"

"Just an educated guess."

Swann stood up from the table.

"Okay," he said. "Thanks for your time."

What he really wanted to do was a step dance on Skiv's head. The punk was almost as bad as Bedard. But Swann figured he might need Skiv again. The connection was good to have, considering Swann's line of work.

"You got another twenty?" Skiv asked as Swann reached the door.

"What for?"

"Grubber and Knickers were real tight. How's that for another connection?"

Swann stared at him for a few moments, then tossed him another bill.

"Hey, this is just a ten, man."

"You're still up twenty from the last time," Swann told him.

He left before Skiv could argue about it. Jess and the other girl were both sitting by the door on the porch when he stepped outside. Swann glanced at Jess.

"Your loverboy's free now," he said.

"Fuck you," she said without any force behind the words. It was like she was saying "good-bye."

Swann shook his head and continued down the steps. When he reached the street he heard Bo's van start up, so he waited for it to pull up in front of him.

"Did you get anything?" Bo asked.

"Well, I learned that everybody's out to fuck everybody else."

"You had to talk to some punks to figure that out?"

Swann shook his head. "No. But it helps to keep it all in perspective."

"You want me to drop you off at Sue's?"

"Sure. And tomorrow we pay a visit to Poirier."

"We're going peacefully — as in no guns?"

"You've got it. You could do me a favour, though."

"Name it."

"Get your reporter friend to see what he can dig up on Don Howland."

"Are we looking for anything in particular?"

"No. Just run the name by him and see what comes up."

Twenty-eight Chapter

Don Howland," Bo said as he slid in across from Swann in Swann's booth at the Avenue.

Swann signalled to Belle for her to bring them coffee.

"So what did you get on him?" he asked.

"Not a helluva lot, Jake."

He pushed a sheet of paper across the table to Swann, then settled back in his seat. Swann ran quickly down the short biography. Howland had been born in Toronto, educated there as well. He was the proverbial self-made man, dealing in real estate, stocks and bonds. Owned an import company that he'd sold in '83 for a tidy profit. Was currently the major money behind a new computer store. He'd been married twice. His first wife died of leukemia. He'd divorced his second in '82. No children.

Swann pushed the paper aside to make room for his coffee as Belle appeared at their table.

"You want some breakfast, Bo?" she asked.

"Just a date."

"We don't have any dates."

"With you, Belle."

She shook her head and grinned. "You never give up, do you?"

"Only when I'm dead, Belle."

He turned in the booth to watch her walk back to the counter.

"One of these days she's going to say yes," Swann said, "and give you a heart attack."

Bo turned back. "If she does, at least I'll die happy."

He added some cream to his coffee and stirred it, then pointed at the sheet on Howland with his spoon.

"So what do you think?"

"He looks clean — but there's room in there for connections."

"I didn't write it down, but besides that place up on the Mountain Road, he owns a bunch of properties in the West End, an apartment building downtown, and some land out around the Perth-Lanark area. You figure he's involved more than Bedard let on?"

"More than Bedard knows, I'd say. I'm willing to bet he hired the guys in the Buick that killed Cohen. And the pair that stopped me in the alley."

"Him and Poirier?"

Swann shook his head. "The hit on Cohen was a stupid move — something Poirier wouldn't pull. It's got the mark of an amateur. Who kills the messenger anymore? Cohen sold as much information to Poirier as he did to the cops and us."

"Howland," Bo said slowly, weighing the name. "I think you're right, Jake. So we're going after him?"

"No. We're still going to talk to Poirier. So finish up that coffee and we'll hit the road."

Bo nodded. "You stash Bedard's boodle?"

"Yeah. I buried it in one of the flowerbeds by the canal — after taking our ten percent handling charge."

"What did that come to?"

"Five grand."

Bo whistled. "I love having my rent paid for half a year by a slimeball like him. You think he'll come across with the Menzies girl?"

"I'll bet he's looking — but I don't figure he'll find her. I don't think he's got her."

"Then who does?"

"Nobody. I think she did go back home — to T.O., anyway — or to Vancouver. I called Brick this morning and he's going to try to run her down for us. If she's on the west coast, he'll find her."

"So we're free to hit Rankin?"

"Only after we talk to Poirier. I want us to be clear of this whole Bedard business with him first. No matter what happens, Bedard's going down, but you can bet Poirier will still be around. Seeing we've got to live in the same city as him, I figure we'd better let him know that we're out of it."

Bo sighed. "Christ, I'd have liked to have had a chance to burn those bastards on this one."

"Remember that place on Cooper Street where you picked me up last night?" Swann asked. "There's a guy named Skiv who lives there. He's the guy that sent the kids to Bedard in the first place. Will he do?"

Bo grinned. "He'll do for now, Jake."

"So you've got something to look forward to. Let's get going."

He paid for his breakfast and Bo's coffee at the cash register and had to push Bo out the door ahead of him as he tried again to make a date with Belle.

"Did you ever see her husband?" Swann asked as they headed for the van.

"Yeah. A skinny little guy — comes up to about my shoulder."

"Everybody comes up to about your shoulder."

"So what about him?"

"He's a black belt. Last guy bugged Belle too much, he put him in the hospital for a week."

Bo looked back at the restaurant. "No shit?"

"No shit."

"I wonder if she's ever thought of divorcing him," Bo said.

Swann shook his head and got into the van.

Twenty-nine

Bo parked the van in front of the tall downtown building that housed Poirier's office. He caught Swann's arm before he could leave the van.

"You sure you want to go up there on your own?" he asked.

Swann nodded. "What's he going to do at this point? I'll give him Howland and see where that takes us."

"Howland might not be enough."

"Poirier needs somebody to take the fall, Bo. Better Howland than you or me. It's not like he isn't up to his ass in it already."

Bo shrugged, plainly unhappy. "If you're not back down in thirty, I'll be coming up, Jake."

"I'll be back."

He went inside the building and took the elevator to the sixteenth floor. One of Poirier's bodyguards stopped him as he stepped out. Like the man accompanying Poirier into The Avenue, he was a big man, all shoulders and arms, casually but neatly dressed in a sports jacket, pressed trousers, beige shirt, tie. The jacket did nothing to hide the bulge under his left armpit.

"Name?" he asked.

"I don't have an appointment," Swann said. "Just tell the man that Swann's here to see him. I think he'll find the time."

The bodyguard nodded. He pushed a buzzer on the wall near the elevator controls. A speaker higher up in the wall crackled and then a voice asked, "Yes?"

"Man here to see Danny, Steve. Says his name is Swann."

"Send him in."

Another buzzer sounded, lower in pitch, and the bodyguard opened the door across from the elevator. Inside the office, a man in a dark grey suit stepped from behind a desk to greet Swann. He was almost Swann's height, but without the body weight. His hair was short, light brown. His face and arms were deeply tanned. The eyes, a startling blue, gave Swann the once-over. The smile on the man's lips never reached his eyes.

"Mr. Swann," he said. "I'm Steve Testa — we talked on the phone."

"Right. Your boss in?"

"Well, you really should have phoned ahead because —"

"Come on, Testa. Cut the crap. Is he in or not? Is he going to see me, or do I take what I've got somewhere else?"

The blue eyes went a couple of degrees cooler. "Come with me."

Swann smiled as Testa ushered him into an office the size of the Avenue Restaurant twice over. It looked more like a penthouse suite, except for the large walnut and glass desk over by a window that looked out on Ottawa's skyline. Swann could see the Parliament Buildings, and behind them, the Ottawa River and Hull. The Gatineaus were a green smudge on the far horizon.

The carpet was plush underfoot and the colour of coffee with double cream. A bar stood in the far corner, sharing that side of the room with a brown leather couch and two leather arm chairs. A glass-topped table with wrought iron legs stood between the chairs. The artwork on the walls was abstract and the paintings were all originals. Two other doors led off on the right side of the room.

Poirier stood up as Swann came in. Swann's gaze went to him, then settled on the vase of flowers on the desk. Poirier caught the look.

"Were you expecting me?" Swann asked with a grin.

"No. But it's a real pleasure to see you, Swann."

"I'll bet. I want to talk to you alone."

Testa looked nervous about leaving Swann alone with his boss, but Poirier waved him out.

"Can I get you something to drink?" he asked as the door closed behind Testa.

"Too early for me."

"Coffee then?"

Swann shook his head. "I don't have a whole lot of time, Poirier, so let's get right down to it."

He crossed the room and laid the sheet of paper that Bo had given him on the desk.

"I'm giving you this," he said.

Poirier sat down and picked it up. "What is it?"

"He's the guy that was backing Bedard — thought the whole thing up in the first place. I traced Bedard down at a place Howland's got up in the Gatineaus."

"Can I talk to Bedard?"

Swann shrugged. "I left him up there last night. Maybe he hung around. But he hasn't got the tapes anymore. I do."

"What do you want for them?"

"Nothing. See, I know you've got your own set, so I just trashed these."

Poirier frowned. He tapped the desk with his fingers. "So what do you want, Swann?"

"I know you were setting me up. You don't have to pretend it was any different. So I'm giving you Howland to take my place. I don't know who it was that got greedy — you or Bedard, or maybe even Howland — and I don't care. All I know is you can have the whole mess. I just want out of it."

"What about the girl you were looking for?"

Swann took a seat across the desk from Poirier and leaned back in it.

"The way I see it, she just split. I'll know for sure in the next couple of days. If I'm wrong, I'll be back sniffing around, but I don't think any of you know where she is."

Poirier nodded. "So now what?"

"Now I walk out of here, you go back to your slimy little businesses, and you leave me and mine alone."

"That's it?"

"Well, you'll owe me one — don't you think?"

"For what?"

"Please — don't get cute, Poirier. Like I said, I know you were setting me up. There's no way you were going to let Bedard get away with fucking you around. I've just given you a much sweeter deal to work with. Silent partner and porn film maker have falling out. It'll sell papers. You own any papers, Poirier?"

"I'm not saying I was setting you up, and I'm not saying I'm interested in doing anything but talk with Marc."

"Fine. I understand. Am I out?"

"Sure. Sure, Swann. Maybe you were never in. Did you ever think of that?"

Swann just smiled and got up out of the chair. "I'll be seeing you around, Poirier. I know the way out."

"One thing, Swann."

Swann turned at the door to look back.

"I never sent anybody out after you."

Swann nodded. "I know that now. Tell me, did you hit Cohen?"

"You nuts? The guy gave me a direct line into more places than anybody else could."

"Then it was Howland."

Swann closed the door on Poirier's frown. Ten minutes later he was with Bo in the van, driving down Bank Street to his apartment. There were two messages waiting for him when he called Sue, one from Brick Morgan, the other from Bedard. He called Brick first, long distance to Vancouver.

"She wasn't that hard to track down," Brick said. "I've got her here in the office with me. Want me to put her on?"

"You didn't go rough on her, did you?"

"What do you think, Jake? All of a sudden I'm a child molester?"

"Okay, okay. Put her on."

There was a moment of silence, then someone clearing their throat. "Mr...uh...Swann?"

"Call me Jake. Is this Patricia Menzies?"

"Yeah. Listen, I came along with your friend because I didn't want any trouble, but you can't just keep me here."

"I don't want to do that."

"I'm *not* going back to my parents."

"I'm not asking you to do that either."

There was a long pause. "Then what...what do you want?"

"I just want to know if you're all right. Do you have a place to stay? Do you have a job?"

"I'm staying with a friend. And I've got a job waitressing in Gas Town. Now you can just tell my father that—"

"Wait a minute, Patricia," Swann broke in. "I'll talk to your father, sure. I've got to. But that's the one thing I want you to do for me. I want you to call him—from Brick's office—as soon as you get off the phone with me."

"But—"

"Just explain things to him like you have to me. You want to tell him why, that's up to you. But all I want is for him to know you're okay. Will you do that?"

"And then what?"

"Then Brick will walk you to the front door of his office, let you out, and tell you to have a nice day."

"That's it?"

"It's not so hard, is it?"

"I guess not."

"The other thing I should tell you is that I know about the films you made here. I've destroyed all the copies of them that I could find, but there might still be some floating around."

"Did you...are you going to tell my father?"

There was a mixture of shame and fear in her voice.

"He hired me to find you," Swann said. "Once you've talked to him, my job's over. I figure anything you did — that's your business. But if you don't mind a little bit of advice, I'd stay away from that kind of thing. It's just going to get you in trouble."

"I...I know. That's why I came here. To get a fresh start."

"I think that's a real good idea. Will you call your parents?"

"They're just going to send somebody else after me if I do."

"Don't you want them to know you're okay?"

"That's why I sent them that card from Ottawa and look what happened — they hired you."

"It could've been worse."

"I suppose."

"You don't have to tell them where you're calling from."

"They'll find out anyway — won't they?"

"Probably. But you're going to have to deal with this someday, Patricia. You might as well get it over with now. Just remember. So long as you're supporting yourself and have a place to stay, they can't touch you. The law's on your side."

"Okay. I'll call."

"Good. You take care now. Will you put Brick back on the line?"

"Sure. Thanks, Mr. Swann. Thanks for not being a pig about all this."

Swann smiled as she got off the phone and passed it back to Brick.

"Send me a bill," he told Brick when the Vancouver detective came back on the line. "This is one I owe you."

"One? Christ, Jake. You're down three or four to me now — but who's counting?"

"Thanks again, Brick. One last thing. Give the kid a couple of hundred dollars and add it to my bill, okay?"

"Do you have that kind of money?" Brick asked.

Swann thought about Bedard's stash. "I'm doing okay," he said. "Catch you later."

He hung up and looked at Bo, then dialed the number Bedard had left with Sue.

"Is she going to be okay?" Bo asked.

"Sure. If she's smart enough to know she's made a mistake and then does something about it, she's smart enough to stay on top of things from here on out. Yeah," he added into the phone as the connection was made. "This is Swann. You left me a message?"

"I can take you to the girl," Bedard said.

"Is it far?"

"Twenty minutes."

"That's great."

"Will you bring the money?"

"Sure. Meet me in half an hour."

Swann gave him the address to Poirier's building.

"But that's Danny's—"

"I know," Swann said and hung up.

"Can you believe the guy?" he asked Bo after he related the brief conversation.

"He probably figured it was worth a try."

"Sure. You set to finish things up?"

Bo nodded. "What about Sammy? She's gonna be pissed if you leave her out of this."

"Maybe I'm wrong, but I don't want her mixed up in this any more than she already has been."

"Makes sense to me. What about the Indian?"

"We'll leave Jimmy to keep an eye on her."

"Okay."

Swann picked up the phone again and dialed Lou Sweet's number.

This is getting to be a bad habit," Lou Sweet said as he got into the passenger's seat of the Acadian. "Maybe you should just make me a partner, Jake, seeing as how we're seeing so much of each other."

"Or at least give you a cut," Swann said as he pulled away from the curb. There was no humour in his voice.

Lou gave him a puzzled look, then turned to look at Bo and Sooey in the back seat. "How's it going, Bo?"

Bo smiled and lifted the barrel of the shotgun he was holding until it pointed straight at Lou's back through the seat.

"Real good, Lou. Now I wouldn't go making any quick moves. Just turn around again, nice and slow. And remember — I can pull this trigger a helluva lot faster than you can get out of that door."

"What the fuck is this?" Lou demanded as he faced front again.

"Maybe you've been living high off the hog for awhile," Swann told him, "but you've always got to pay up in the end."

"I don't know what you assholes are playing at, but it's not funny."

"No joke, Sweet."

Lou let out a long breath.

"Okay," he said. "What's going on, Jake?"

His voice was even, his anger just barely held in check.

"Maybe we could start with where you were last Friday night," Swann said.

"Why?"

Bo hit the back of the seat with the shotgun.

"Just answer the question," he said.

"I was at Maria's. Listen, Jake. We've been friends for a long time. If you've got something going down—"

"Shut up," Swann told him.

He shot Lou a quick glance, then returned his gaze to the road.

"I don't want to hear about what fucking good friends we've been. I'll tell you, Sweet. We know all about you and your deals with Poirier. You and your pal Rankin. Thing we want to know is, were you with him the night he did his little number on Sammy? Or did you just stand back and cover his ass?"

"Oh, Jesus, Jake. You've got this all wrong. I'm—"

"I don't want to hear any more lies, Sweet. You don't know Rankin, you told me, but I saw you being awfully buddy-buddy with him last Saturday night. With him and Weppler. And we know who Weppler works for."

"Christ, Swann. I can explain that. I told you we're running an investigation on Rankin."

"So you figured socializing with him was a good way to make points?"

"Fercrissakes! I'm trying to bust the bastard. The only way I can find out how deep he's in and who's with him is by going over to his side. You think I like sucking up to that slimeball?"

"I don't know, Sweet."

Swann didn't like the way this was going. Everything had seemed cut and dried just a few moment ago.

"Maybe we should listen to him," Bo said.

Swann glanced in the rearview mirror. Bo looked worried.

"I don't know," Swann said. "I've been handed so much bullshit for the past few days that everything smells to me."

"I'm telling you, Swann," Lou said. "You fuck this up and I'll have your balls."

"We'll see. We'll see where you were on Friday night. Then we'll see what Rankin's got to say about you."

He pulled over to the side of the road beside a phone booth and killed the engine. Reaching over, he relieved Lou of his .38.

"Watch him," he told Bo.

He got out, went to the phone booth, and called Maria at Statistics Canada where she worked. Bo and Lou watched him talk on the phone, hang up, then dial another number. He talked a little longer the second time, then finally returned to the car.

"Okay," he said. "You're clean for Friday, but we've still got Rankin to talk to."

"He's on duty."

"I set up a meet at his place in three quarters of an hour."

"Swann, you are fucking up royally."

Swann turned to look at him.

"If Rankin did to Maria what he did to Sammy, would you be singing the same song?"

"I..."

"Just think about it," Swann said.

He started up the Acadian, grinding the starter when the engine coughed into life. Lou sat limp in his seat and just stared out the window as they drove to Riverview Park. No one spoke until they pulled into Rankin's lane.

"I spent two months putting this together," Lou said. "It's taking you about two hours to fuck it up for good."

"Just look at it as one of the vagaries of your profession," Swann said. "Come on. Let's get out. I want to be waiting inside when Rankin shows."

He held Lou's .38 on him while Bo got out. Not until Lou was standing on the driveway with Bo covering him, did Swann join them himself. Bo kept the shotgun by his leg so that any watching neighbours wouldn't get too curious. Swann led the way to the front door, keeping out of Bo's line of fire. Sticking the .38 into his belt, he got out his picks and bent over the door to work on the lock. As he did, the front door opened and he looked into the barrel of a .357 Magnum.

Swann stood up slowly to face the weapon's owner. The man was Bo's height, not quite as meaty, but solid looking. He wore a T-shirt that said "Cops do it better" and a pair of jeans. His blonde hair was short, his features roughly chiselled — perfect for a beer commercial. He smiled as he took in the three of them.

"Tell your friend to lay down the shotgun," he said as he plucked the .38 from Swann's belt.

Swann turned slowly to tell Bo when the man hit him hard in the kidney. The pain from the blow was just registering when something struck him hard across the back of his head and he crumpled to the walk.

"Bring him in," the man said, pointing the Magnum at Lou and Bo.

Bo laid the shotgun on the grass very carefully, then went to give Lou a hand with Swann's limp body. Behind in the Acadian, Sooey was barking, but the windows were rolled up high and he couldn't get out. Whining, the dog watched the men disappear into the house.

I n the fall of 1982, Swann ran a man named Gaston Lemire off Highway 8, on the section that runs between Aylmer and Quyon.

Swann was driving an old Chev that night, Lemire a Ford pickup. Swann passed him going south, after spending the better part of the evening tailing him, then just cranked the wheel to his right and ran Lemire right off the road. There was no ditch, just a steep incline.

The pickup rolled down the slope and crashed sideways into a pair of old oak trees. Unlike television, there was no fiery explosion. Lemire had survived, but he spent three months in the hospital, another in therapy, and he still didn't walk right. Which was more than could be said for Nick Panchuk.

Nick had been a friend of Swann's that Lemire had run off the same road two months earlier. Nick hadn't survived his crash.

If it had been just an accident, Swann could have lived with his pain and let it go. But Lemire was a self-professed tough guy, working out of Hull, and word came back to Swann of him bragging how he'd killed this guy who'd been making time with his girl, so don't any of you *maudit* bastards get any ideas of trying it yourselves. Nobody made time with Gaston Lemire's girl.

It didn't matter to Lemire that the woman in question wouldn't even talk to him. It didn't matter to Swann either, except after that night on Highway 8 there was nobody around to chase off her prospective boyfriends.

In the thirty-three months since that night, Swann had thought a lot about what he'd done — the right and wrong of it, and the fact that he'd probably do the same thing again, if circumstances warranted it. He'd tried to ease back on the kinds of cases that could put him or his friends into that kind of situation again. Nick had been running down some leads for Swann when he'd met Gaston Lemire's so-called girlfriend.

Swann had concentrated on insurance frauds, doing legwork for lawyers, simple jobs, but his specialty was dealing with lowlifes and invariably that was the kind of case that came his way. He'd had his first run-in with Danny Poirier in the summer of 1983. Until the past weekend, that was the closest he'd come to the kind of anger that burned dully inside him ever since the brutal attack on Sammy Ward.

There was right and wrong in the world and Swann was one of those men who didn't believe in the grey areas. He didn't really care about what the world did, just so long as no one messed around with him, his friends, or his clients. It was a simple enough way to live, until the past few days when he'd discovered that Lou Sweet was lying to him.

Lou's betrayal had thrown a cloud of doubt over the way Swann viewed the world. It upset the balance of black and white, leaving him with an emptiness inside, a hurt as deep as the one he felt for Sammy. It had sent him recklessly risking both his own and Bo's lives last night. It had done the same again today.

He understood that now as his eyes flickered open and the blurry images of both Lou and Bo handcuffed to chairs came into focus. He was lying on a carpeted floor. He didn't move, didn't want to give himself away. The pain in the back of his head was a sharp throb that he used to clear his mind of any lingering doubts. The man hadn't hit him in the same place that he'd gotten sapped the other night, but it was close enough to make no difference. If he didn't come up with something soon, he figured that they'd all be suffering from a lot worse than that.

A strange sense of peace settled in him when he realized that Lou was handcuffed as well as Bo. He was going to have to make it up to Lou for having doubted him, but right at the moment it didn't really seem to matter. It was enough that Lou hadn't betrayed him.

So far as he could tell, he hadn't been handcuffed himself. But he wasn't sure he could trust himself to stand, little say do anything else at the moment. His headache was a knife going in and out of his head. His throat was dry, thick feeling. Given a choice, he'd prefer to just lie here until it all went away. The hot and cold flashes. The dryness. The pain.

He steeled himself to move, but before he could, the soft murmur of voices he'd been vaguely aware of approached and grew louder. He forced himself to relax and stay limp as the voices came in the room.

"Well, Lou," one of them said. "You were good enough to sucker your friends, but not good enough to get by us."

"A cop like you, Rankin, just makes me—"

"Yeah, yeah. Spare me the theatrics. We had you figured out from when you first approached us, you know? I mean, the commission should have picked somebody at least a little tarnished if they'd wanted to get anywhere. But the first thing I thought when True-Blue Lou, the career cop, came knocking on my door is, it's a fix. Then I sat down and worked out how I could turn it to my advantage. So all the time you figured you were getting your in with us, we've been setting you up, Lou. How do you like that?"

"What do you mean?"

"Oh, it's sweet—just like you, Lou. Thanks to Weppler and a certain bank manager that his people have in their pocket, we've got records connecting you to organized crime that go back about seven years. Nice little monthly payments of a grand, with the occasional extra payoff that'll look like a bonus. The account's been all set up — withdrawals, the automatic deposits.

"And where does the money go? Well, if you could see your place, Lou. We're replacing a few of your things — your stereo, your TV, that kind of shit — with real state-of-the-art equipment. Plus, there'll be some investment information and references to a bookie where you maybe lost a little more bread than a guy like you can earn honestly.

"Starting to get the picture, Lou? And now, well, things got a little hot, so you decided to go to the commission and set me and a couple of my friends up to take the fall for you, only we got wise. You came after us, with a couple of pals along for the ride, and decided to take us down. Unfortunately, we were too good for you and you and your pals didn't quite survive the encounter. How do you like the story so far, Lou?"

"You'll never get away with it."

"Oh, Jesus. Don't feed me those fucking clichés. The only place nobody gets away with it is on all those cop shows on TV. This is real life, Lou. And in real life, the good guys always get the shaft."

"The commission came to *me*. They'll investigate — they'll find you out."

"Well, maybe they'll hassle me a bit. I could even lose my badge, but I'll tell you, Lou, I'm getting awfully tired of this badge anyway. Used to be, you could get a little respect with it. Nowadays, the only respect you get is what you beat into somebody's head."

"Your father was a good cop," Lou said. "But you — "

"My father was a sucker — just like you, Lou. Forty-three years on the force and what did it get him? The only friends he had were cops, and talk about your small minds. Jesus Christ. He was three months in the hospital, wasting away, and how many of them do you think bothered to come by?"

"That's why you're selling out your badge?"

"Fuck no. I'm just plain greedy, Lou. I want it all."

Swann opened his eyes a crack and studied the scene through his lashes. Rankin was standing with his back towards Swann, facing Lou. The other man had to be behind him then. He saw Bo looking at him, realizing he was conscious. Bo gave an almost imperceptible shake of his head. Swann ignored him and tried to figure just where Rankin's partner would be standing. He knew he had to do something and quick. Rankin was winding down. He'd be making his play any time now. Before he did, Swann had to make his own. He wouldn't get another chance.

He just wasn't sure he could trust his body to do what he told it. He'd been hit before. He remembered how woozy he'd been when he'd gotten sapped the other night. A ten-year-old could have knocked him down with a finger.

He had to centre himself, focus on what he wanted. He had to be up and moving and never mind his body's weakness.

Rankin wasn't armed. The man behind Swann would be. Covering his partner. That was one of the first things a cop learned: you always covered your partner.

Focus.

He wanted Rankin.

He brought Sammy's face up in his mind's eye — the way she'd looked Saturday afternoon when he'd first seen her. Lying there in the bed. Like a broken doll.

Rankin.

The good guys always get the shaft, Rankin had said.

But that was only when they played by the rules.

"If I was coming to get you," Lou said, "I'd be coming with my own men — not these guys."

"Only if you were on the up and up," Rankin said. "But you were fixing to frame me, see? So you brought these two clowns with you."

Rankin turned and stepped closer to Swann. It had to be now.

"You see," Rankin said, "you've got to —"

Swann moved. He was up off the floor, grabbing Rankin, before the dizziness hit him like a blow. Concentrating on his focus, he heaved Rankin bodily at the gunman he knew was standing behind them, turning as he did so.

Rankin careened into the gunman, throwing him to one side. Swann stumbled towards them, trying to get his vision to clear. The problem was, he wasn't seeing double. There were two gunmen.

The second man fired. His shot went high, hitting Swann in the shoulder, spinning him half around. By the time the man fired again, Swann was right on top of him, batting the gun aside.

The second shot went off into the floor at their feet.

Before he could fire a third time, Swann hit the man across the throat, hard enough to break his windpipe.

He fell across the gunman as the gunman collapsed. He tried to grab for the gun with his left hand, but that arm wouldn't work properly. He landed on top of the gunman, the weapon trapped between their bodies. Waves of sickness washed over him. His shoulder was on fire. His head filled with a white heat.

He clawed for the gun with his right hand, turning to see Rankin moving towards him. Behind Rankin, the first gunman had recovered and was levelling his Magnum at Swann.

Then Bo, dragging the armchair that one of his arms was handcuffed to across the room, hauled off and hit the gunman with his free hand. The gunman was driven back against the wall. He tried to bring up his Magnum, but Bo kicked him in the groin, then chopped down on the exposed back of the gunman's neck. The man dropped to the floor.

Swann's fingers closed on the second man's weapon. Before he could haul it free, Rankin kicked him in the side. As he moved in closer to kick Swann again, Swann finally dragged the gun out. He backhanded Rankin across the side of the head with the barrel of the gun, the sights tearing a bloody gouge from his cheek that cut to the bone.

Rankin moved a step back. Swann looked up at him from where he lay. All he wanted to do was stop fighting the pain and go with it to wherever it would take him. Maybe to Lisdoonvarna, like Sammy'd said she'd done.

His vision was blurring. He saw Rankin as a smudge.

"You remember Friday night?" he asked the smudge. "The girl you had your fun with?"

Little gremlins made of fire were crawling through his body, tap-dancing in his head. He concentrated on keeping the gun steady.

"What about her?" Rankin asked. He was starting to edge forward again.

"Swann, no!" Lou roared.

"This is for her," Swan said and he pulled the trigger.

Bo moved to one side as the bullet hit Rankin. The force of it lifted Rankin to his toes and threw him three feet back. It blew a hole the size of a football out of his back before depositing him in a heap on the man that Bo had taken out. The recoil lifted Swann's arm up and the weapon spun out of his slackening grip.

He looked up to see Bo's face as the big man's features loomed over him. Bo worked the keys to the handcuffs free from the pocket of the man under Swann. Unlocking his own, he tossed the keys to Lou, then bent over Swann again.

"Jesus," he muttered. "You got a death wish or something, Jake?"

Swann wanted to come up with something snappy to say, but it was all he could do to make out Bo's features in the blur that was before his eyes. In the end, he gave up and just let himself go into the darkness where the pain couldn't follow.

Thirty-two

Swann awoke in a hospital room similar to the one he'd found Sammy in, except he seemed to have lucked out and gotten a private room immediately. He stared up at the ceiling, a little surprised to even be opening his eyes. There was natural light coming through the window, so it had to be at least a day after the fiasco at Rankin's place.

A death wish, he remembered Bo saying.

Maybe Bo was right. Sane people didn't get themselves into that kind of situation in the first place.

He turned his head towards the window and realized for the first time that he wasn't alone.

"Thank God," Sammy said. "You're back. I was so scared."

"I thought you were the one in the hospital," Swann said.

"If you ever pull a stunt like that again, you big lummox, I'll…"

Swann smiled briefly as her voice trailed off.

"Nobody uses the word lummox anymore," he told her.

Bo and Jimmy Crackle appeared behind her.

"I figured you could afford a single room," Bo said, "considering the terrible accident that happened to Bedard."

"What happened?"

"Seems he and his silent partner Howland had a falling out and wasted each other."

"Nice and neat."

"For Poirier, anyway."

"What about yesterday?" Swann asked.

"Well, Lou's pissed as hell, but seeing how you saved his ass — not to mention his rep — he's backing you all the way. There's gonna be an inquiry, but things are pretty clear-cut. Rankin didn't have time to tidy up his own trail too well."

"His friends?"

"The one you hit's dead. The other guy's alive, but hurting. They also pulled in two others. Unfortunately, Poirier has *his* ass covered, so all the Crown's getting is some crooked cops."

"With you as the hero," Jimmy Crackle said.

"That's bullshit."

"That's okay," Bo said. "It'll still be great for business. Of course you *can* afford to take a holiday."

"You dug up Bedard's money?"

"I wasn't going to leave it there for some NCC workman to find. I thought we'd split it five ways — what do you think?"

"Sounds good. Maybe I'll take a trip."

Swann looked at Sammy.

"I've been thinking," he said. "Did you ever feel like going to that big festival they have in Ireland every year? It's in some little village in County Clare..."

Sammy's eyes lit up. "You and me?"

Swann nodded.

"Lisdoonvarna," Sammy breathed. "Just try and keep me away."

Jimmy Crackle smiled.

"Looks like someone finally managed to knock some sense into his head," he said to Bo.

They left the room as Sammy leaned forward to kiss Swann. Bo paused in the doorway and looked back.

"I'll tell Sue to hold your calls," he said, but neither of them was listening.